The Bull Chop

Jude Linsey is a young man who is content to live off his rich father's allowance. He ekes out the money in and out of Spooner's Drift by gambling, or fishing and hunting beaver in the high creeks of Shell Mountain. Then the town's bank gets robbed, and Jude is suddenly aware there's a chance to redeem himself with his family and friends. But the deceitful Sheriff Ingram Bere had to be considered: a man with a covetous eye and more than a lawful interest in Jude's welfare.

To mull over his predicament, Jude takes to the timberline with his saddle-broke roan. But events change, and Jude has little choice but to pit his wits and guns against Bart and Dooley Susans' gang of hard-nosed, desperate killers.

The Bull Chop

ABE DANCER

A Black Horse Western

ROBERT HALE · LONDON

ISBN 978-0-7090-8492-1

Robert Hale Limited
Clerkenwell House
Clerkenwell Green
London EC1R 0HT

www.halebooks.com

Typeset by
Derek Doyle & Associates, Shaw Heath
Printed and bound in Great Britain by
Antony Rowe Limited, Wiltshire

1

The Bull Chop was a broad curving valley of thirty miles in length from north to south. For nearly twenty miles on its westerly side, where the hills rolled away from thick-timbered canyons, fat trout held swim positions in the brooks and creeks. It was at the northern end that rich grassland provided perfect cattle range.

From where Leo Grainger watched quietly, the valley narrowed into a two-mile wide strip. Two creeks ran together to make the main stream that drained Bull Chop, then headed off through a broken landscape, westward towards Rio Dell Scotia, Humboldt Bay and the Pacific Ocean.

The only town in the valley was Spooner's Drift, situated with its straggling outskirts almost reaching the edge of the timber beneath Shell Mountain. The town derived its business mainly from horse and cattle dealing, and the ranches of the valley were small when considering the open hills to the south-west and the vast country to the north.

Spooners – as it was known locally – had its main street, two that flanked parallel, and half a dozen that intersected them. In the middle of town was the small brick courthouse with a few fir and madrona trees supplying shade for its plaza. Back of this court-house was where the gallows was erected when a horse-thief or murderer had to be hanged.

At the north end of First Street was a single span bridge that crossed Eel Creek, a watercourse that had its head in the innumerable springs and creeks off the mountain. Beyond this bridge and a ways off the wagon road was a large corral where horse and cattle sales were made, where wild range mustangs were occasionally broken.

Around noon on a hot Saturday in August, Leo Grainger had driven into town from his ranch in the fold of hills to the south-west. Running behind his buggy was a sturdy, arched-necked roan gelding that snorted and swerved from side to side, rolled its eyes at every new thing it saw. Its lead rope had been fash-ioned with a choker hitch, and the horse had learned there was little to be gained in trying to break loose during the ten-mile trip from the LG ranch.

A lone mourning dove fluttered on to a nearby rooftop, called low and furtively until another one landed alongside. The birds measured each other in silence while the whole covey made a circle in the sun before alighting in a line along the parapet of the next building. The doves eyed the ranchers, buckaroos and idlers alike who were sitting on the steps of the Blue Coop Saloon below them.

'What you goin' to do with that roan, Leo?' one of the men called out. 'Anyone with half an eye open can see he's a durned outlaw. You here to sell him?'

Grainger stopped his sweat-caked bay in front of the saloon. He stroked his gingery beard and looked about him thirstily.

'Yeah, There's nobody at my ranch can ride him.'

Men who looked as though they knew and understood horse flesh, half circled the roan. They kept at a distance, made savvy remarks about the long bones, the Roman nose and wild rolling eyes.

'You could've hitched him in with a six-horse team. That's been known to take the stuffin' out of 'em,' a man called Turkel suggested.

'Yeah, I heard that's what you did with your missus,' Grainger said with a leery smile. He climbed from the buggy, asked a fat, doughy-faced boy to hold the bay.

He went into the saloon and had a whiskey, quickly followed it with another. It mellowed him as he chewed over the problem of how to sell the roan for more than its worth when there wasn't a man in the whole valley who could ride it.

When Grainger went back to the boardwalk he casually puffed on his cheap cigar, contemplated the growing crowd around the horse.

'What you willin' to pay for someone to saddle break it?' an acquaintance wanted to know.

'Ten dollars comes to mind,' Grainger said. 'That's a fair sum for here an' now.'

'Huh, I sure wouldn't want to ride that hellion for less than twenty,' remarked the young fatster who'd held on to the bay for ten minutes.

'You wouldn't want to ride him, *period*,' Grainger advised, with a good-humoured shake of his head. 'He'd buck you up there with them doves. But perhaps there's someone who'd like to buy him from me. He's got the makin's of a damn fine cow pony.'

'I'll give you twenty-five dollars, Leo,' Aldo Beecher said. The man didn't actually have the dollars, but strangely enough he did own a small ranch.

'No,' Grainger declined. 'The feller who gets this geldin' will have to dig a lot deeper than that. Let's start at one hundred.'

'Thirty,' offered another man. 'It'll probably cost that much again to break him, an' nobody knows what he'll be worth after that.'

'Forty,' shouted Beecher, who'd decided that he might be able to make a work horse out of the roan.

Grainger smiled. 'Here we got a horse o' real promise. He just needs a firm but carin' hand to get him there,' he explained tolerantly.

There was another bid of fifty dollars and he

refused with a snort. 'Don't any o' you goddamn hay shakers know a horse that rips, when you see it?'

'There you go talkin' down Turkel's missus again,' someone teetered out. 'No, Leo, we reckon you're just tryin' to work off an outlaw on us. Problem is, most of us ain't fool enough to buy.'

During all this bartering and raillery, a tall, muscular young man had lolled quietly against the wall of the Blue Coop. His hands were rammed into his pants pockets, and he'd dragged his Stetson sombrero down over his grey eyes. He was Jude Linsey, son of one of the town's wealthier merchants. The most irresponsible man in Spooner's Drift was also well liked, carried a smile that made friends quickly. Mainly he hunted, fished and explored the mountains, sometimes as far north as Eagle Point. He could easily get a job on any ranch where a top hand was needed, *if* he'd wanted that sort of work. Jude had once worked three months for Leo Grainger, but, true to form, he'd quit just when Grainger was thinking he'd stay.

'Howdy, Jude,' Grainger called out. 'You workin' steady yet?'

With one finger, Jude pushed his hat up an inch. 'Nope,' he said. 'Ain't got the time.' Then he nodded at the roan. 'I remember that mean son-of-a-bitch.'

Grainger wanted to say that since Jude had last seen the gelding, it had done some wagon work and been introduced to a saddle. But he knew that Jude was a better judge of horses than he was of any tall tale.

'I wouldn't do this for anyone but you, Jude,' he confided, 'but I'll let you have the roan for the very special, one-day-only price o' seventy-five dollars. That's at least twenty less than he's worth, an' you goddamn know it.'

'That's a fact, Mr.Grainger, an' I'd sure like to have him,' Jude said. 'But I ain't carryin' that sort o' money today.'

'Then you can take him on time pay,' Grainger suggested, 'or go see your pa.'

For a short moment Jude's eyes flashed cold. 'I got a better idea. Do you want to bet real money that there ain't a man in town can stay on him for three minutes?' he suddenly proposed.

'Hell no,' Grainger replied quickly. 'But startin' with *you*, I might lay a *small* sum. You want to try for fifty?' Having recently picked up a few hundred dollars from the sale of a small herd of beef cattle, Grainger was feeling the twinge of a temperate gambler.

Jude grinned mischievously. 'I might be able to raise a worthwhile stake . . . an incentive to keep me stuck on him,' he said. He knew of Grainger's sale, felt that he was owed some of it. For the time he'd spent at the LG ranch, he felt he'd done more than twice the work he'd been paid for. 'But I reckon my neck's worth a lot more'n fifty dollars,' he said. 'So, I guess you'll just have to take the geldin' back home.'

'Make it a hundred then,' Grainger offered with a shade more enthusiasm.

'Naagh, I'm just joshin' you. I'm not really sure I could stick on that geldin' for more'n one minute for *any* amount,' Jude cajoled.

Grainger pulled a skin poke and shook it invitingly in front of Jude. 'Two hundred dollars says you can't stay in the saddle for two minutes. My final offer.'

Jude gave the impression he was considering the wager, when the sheriff arrived. Attracted by the unusually agitated crowd in front of the Blue Coop, Ingram Bere had walked over from the courthouse. He was burly, no more than forty years of age and sported a large, drooping moustache. Several people in the crowd knew how easy it would be to start trouble between Jude and the sheriff. They knew that Bere found it difficult to hide his attraction for Alice Rickson.

'A hundred dollars a minute is a mighty good rate o' pay, Mr. Grainger,' Jude Linsey now responded. 'It'll take me a moment to match it, o' course.'

There were a chuckles from some of the men in the crowd. They knew that Jude had never owned $200 at any time in his life, in spite of the fact that his father was rich.

It was generally agreed that Jude should attempt to ride the roan at midday. The arrangement suited Grainger's plan, in as much as he could put the roan in the livery stable for a light feed of oats and barley.

A mix that would stimulate the horse, give it the vigour to shoot its back.

'An' just where're *you* goin' to raise two hundred bucks?' Sheriff Bere mocked as he stepped towards the younger man. 'No one with any sense would loan you a rope if you were drownin' in horse piss.'

Jude's icy smile returned. He lifted his right arm and roughly pushed the flat of his hand up against the sheriff's reddening face.

'Only *one* person,' he said angrily as Bere spluttered. 'An' I'd rather drown than take it.'

Bere tottered backwards and tried to regain his balance. 'You shouldn'ta laid a hand on me, you . . . your . . .' he started. He lurched forward, but Jude side-stepped, and he stumbled on. He put out a hand, but couldn't stop himself from colliding with the low frame of the saloon.

Unsteadily, Bere moved sideways. He put a hand up to feel where he'd barked the skin from the bridge of his big fleshy nose. Together with the crowd, Jude was waiting for the sheriff to recover his balance. They'd all stepped back to leave room for the ensuing street fight.

'I swear the law's goin' to take care o' you,' Bere vowed as he glared vengefully at Jude.

'There's too many folk here for you to risk harmin' me through your tin star, Sheriff. You want to go around buttin' walls, that's your affair,' Jude said with grating nonchalance.

'I don't need any goddamn badge of office to

whup you, Linsey. An' as sure as I'm standin' here, there's goin' to be another time.'

'That'll be worth bookin' a seat for,' a man whispered to his neighbour. 'I'll go an' ask the missy Alice if she fancies makin' a wager on the outcome, haw haw.'

2

Jude Linsey went to see his father in the mercantile, to ask for a loan of $200.

'What do you want it for?' the elder Linsey, demanded to know. 'To gamble with, or some other idiotic use?'

Briefly, Jude explained his meeting with Leo and the roan.

'Huh, I might've known. Haven't you got any bigger ambition than ridin' some wild horse?'

'Ridin' *that* wild horse *is* ambitious,' Jude answered. 'An' if I *do* ride him, it's an easy way to pick up a couple o' hundred.

Jude's father turned away, shook his head disappointedly. 'Sorry, Jude. But all you're gettin' from me is your monthly allowance. Any more, an' you can work it off. That's normal for other folk.'

'Ridin' an outlaw bronc is work. It's only a gamble 'cause o' the way you're lookin' at it.

'You're chosin' the wastrel's road, Jude. I told your

14

mother as much.'

'I ain't a store man, Pa, an' never will be; get used to it. I want to buy an' sell *cattle*, not buttons an' bows.'

With that, Jude sauntered back out of the store. He went to see Corbet Welt who owned and ran the Blue Coop Saloon.

Welt chuckled behind his long, slim beard. 'Sure you can have it,' he said. 'You think you can ride that bangtail?'

'Yeah, I've an idea I can.'

'Well, the business I'm in, that's good enough, Jude. I'd even like to get along to see it. By the way, I hope you shook hands with the sheriff after slappin' him around.'

'I didn't slap him.'

'Oh? Well it sounded like it was as good as, an' in front of most o' the town. Don't sound like the smartest thing you ever done with your right hand, Jude. Even if Bere didn't have some sort o' personal antagonism towards you, he certainly does *now*.' Welt tapped the side of his nose suggestively. 'An' it ain't the sort o' behaviour that'll sit easy with ol' Forbes Rickson, if you know what I mean.'

Jude gave a thin smile. 'Yeah I know that,' he agreed. 'But I ain't much carin' at the moment. I got other stuff to attend to.'

Slightly before midday, there were nearly fifty people at the round corral just north of the creek. Many of them were perched along the top rail, and there were quite a few women and children.

'What we here for, Pa?' a little boy was asking.

'The rodeo's come to town,' the father answered hopefully.

The general hubbub didn't help the temperament of the roan. It was trotting slowly round and round the corral looking for a place where it might make its escape. Then it shied towards the middle, stopped rolling its eyes to stare balefully at its surroundings.

The men who were pressed against the gate, moved away when Jude came forward. He was wearing hickory shirt and pants, carried a high-cantled saddle, a bridle, a thick saddle blanket and a braided hackamore. He dropped the gear at the base of a fence pole, drew a forty-foot reata from its loop on the saddle and slowly ran it through his hands.

Leo Grainger, perched on the fence not far from the gate, was soon disturbed by the look of Jude's unhurried assurance. He was also thinking of what he'd tell his wife if by some chance he lost the $200 bet.

'Now let's make sure we got this straight, Leo,' Jude called out to him. 'I've got to stick on this gut twister for two minutes . . . no longer?'

'Yeah,' Grainger said, the uncertainty growing. 'Two goddamn minutes.'

Cash money in such a basic, rough-edged part of the country was scarce among the spectators, and bets of little more than one and two dollars were now being made all round the corral.

Jude ran a loop into the reata, started a slow walk towards the snorting, high-headed horse. The roan began to retreat, first at a walk, then a more nervous trot. It swung its muscular hind quarters so close to the fence, that a startled spectator toppled from the rails. Jude didn't follow in the roan's tracks, but in a smaller circle, as the horse broke into a wild, snorting gallop. Jude let the animal charge madly around and around the corral. Then, as it came around the third time, he shot out the loop close to the ground, directly in the roan's path.

The horse stamped its forefeet in the loop and Jude quickly heeled himself backwards, turning the rope around his waist. The next moment, the roan let out a fiery grunt, as it hit the corral's layer of deep soft dust. Before it could scramble back to its feet, Jude had a knee pressed close to its jugular. A moment later, he had the other end of his rope around the smallest part of its neck.

'Hey!' the man called Turkel yelled out. 'You're supposed to ride it, not measure it up for a set o' store boughts.'

'Or maybe he ain't the skim-milker we all thought,' someone retorted.

There were a few onlookers who'd been offering small bets on Jude not being able to last out the two requisite minutes. But that increased when Ingram Bere started up.

'If there's anyone interested, I'll take on all the

money that's offered, that he can't ride that brute,' he yelled. The sheriff wasn't going to miss out on the chance of Jude Linsey coming a cropper, maybe with broken bones to boot.

After all the initial betting, there wasn't much in the way of extra wagering money left to the assembled crowd. But after some talking and pocket-searching, Bere managed to get twenty dollars of his money covered.

By this time, Jude had the roan scrambling to its feet, had led it shying towards the gate, where spectators backed off sharply. He had to do his own saddling, but on the one or two occasions he'd attempted to ride the roan out at Leo Grainger's ranch, he'd got to understand something of the horse's spirit. He threw a reata loop around the Roman nose, drew the horse away from the fence and dropped the loose end of the rawhide rope to the ground.

The horse remained very still and Jude held up his hand. 'You folks just keep nice an' quiet,' he said. 'This feller ain't broke yet.' Then he picked up and smoothed out his saddle blanket.

'Is that buffalo?' Aldo Beecher asked him.

'Yeah,' Jude said. 'I got no need to hurt him without good cause.' He set the blanket gently on the back of the roan, adjusted it carefully. Knowing the time for protest was when Jude took to the saddle, the horse offered no protest. But it breathed hard when Jude gently laid the saddle on to the thick blanket.

Jude carefully shifted the saddle high on the withers, then stretched to push the hackamore under the roan's chin. With one quick movement, he then reached under the horse and grabbed the end of the cinch. He knew that this was when a snorty horse could likely swing its neck down to chomp on a man's arm, or neck even.

Clutching the end of the hackamore with his left hand, Jude slotted the end of the latigo through the upper and lower cinch rings. He drew gently, eased the saddle back down to a more secure and settled position on the roan's back, before a final tighten.

Then he let go of the hackamore and with a little gentle breaking patter, unrolled the near-side stirrup.

'For Chris'sakes,' Turkel yelled. 'Are you goin' to play around with that horse all day? Or are you just waitin' for Miss Rickson to get here?'

Jude cursed under his breath, and walked slowly over to the fence. 'You open your mouth again, mister, an' I'll push my boot into it, leg an' all,' he shared confidentially with the man.

'Get on with it, Jude. I got to get back to the ranch before full dark,' Grainger shouted.

'Yeah, if you ain't goin' to ride, just say so,' Ingram Bere pitched in from the far side of the corral. 'I for one am gettin' tired o' your stallin' an' four-flushin'.'

Jude looked across at Bere, eyed him thoughtfully for a moment, then walked slowly back to the roan.

The horse's head was now slightly drooped, as if it might be taking a brief, standing nap.

Jude walked slowly around the head of the horse, looked it in the eye, then went on to pick up his bridle. With more reassuring sounds, he fitted it, pulled the reins over the dark, gleaming neck and carefully untied and discarded the reata. For another minute, the horse continued to flatten its ears while Jude rubbed its trembling shoulders.

3

When Forbes Rickson reached the top of the grade and failed to see his daughter ahead of him, he wasn't much worried. He would find her in town, and then he'd attempt to end her romance with that cock o' the plain, Jude Linsey.

But at the moment Rickson had something else on his mind beside Alice. Along with other prominent townsfolk, he was worried about the Susan Boys, a small but fast-moving gang that for the last two years had been robbing banks and trains along the route of the Great Northern Rail Road. At Cottonwood they'd fired on the law; at Arbuckle they'd shot and killed an elderly man who'd thrown up his arms in a brave, but mistaken attempt to stop them.

Rickson was a stockholder of the Spooner's Drift Bank and, as such, he had a $500 mortgage on his range at the head of the valley. He benefited from stockholder's gains, but he'd also be liable for any losses. Besides, any raid would wipe out the cash used in checking accounts. And he couldn't withdraw *his* cash, such as it was, for fear of the bank foreclosing on him; a disaster, because his ranch and its land was now worth nearly six times that amount.

'Five thousand goddamn dollars never seemed so much before,' he seethed, and flicked his whip out from the rig.

Rickson was halfway to town when he sighted his daughter. She was far ahead to the south on a high stretch of the road, and it immediately altered his troubled thinking.

For some months, it seemed to him, Alice had acted foolishly and impulsively over that worthless Jude Linsey. She had refused to listen to any of his advice about finding a capable and trustworthy husband-to-be.

'Like Sheriff Bere,' Alice had said, in a tired and uninterested comeback.

But Rickson had replied, 'Why yes, actually. If them Susan Boys do attempt to rob our bank – heaven help us – perhaps you'd see what Ingram Bere's really made of.'

'I already know,' Alice had countered, before adding 'lard', under her breath.

Rickson cursed. He'd been gaining on his daughter, but now he noticed she was pulling further away. 'She's seen me, wants to get close to Linsey before I do,' he reasoned to no one but himself.

Alice had looked back a few times, but knew full well who it was following. Her immediate reaction was to lift her spurs to the flanks of her buckskin, because she wanted to know why there was such a crowd gathered around the horse corral at the north end of town. From less than a half-mile away, she sent her horse down the long slope, then splashed through the creek and out on to the levels.

'Miss Alice is comin',' someone said. 'Looks like Turkel weren't such a ways off beam, after all.'

'Yeah, now perhaps we'll get to see a ride,' Aldo Beecher suggested.

Alice's mount sent dirt and gravel flying. She pulled to a stop within feet of where some folk were trying to get a good view. She was going to yell for Jude's attention, but saw that Ingram Bere was coming alongside. The sheriff placed a hand on the buckskin's hip, and Alice looked down, was interested in his seemingly hesitant approach.

'In case you get to wonderin', or hear about it from someone else, Alice, me an' Jude had a difference of opinion. But it weren't much, an' its over now,' Bere said.

Before Alice could ask him if Jude riding the wild roan was anything to do with it, a yell came from the people who'd turned back to watch. Alice moved them aside as she heeled hard, turning her mount closer in to the corral.

'He ain't stallin' any longer,' Beecher said. 'Let the games begin.'

As Jude swung powerfully to the saddle, the roan arched its back for a buck jump. But instead it suddenly shook itself, went into a dazed and uncertain shuffle.

'Rowel him,' a man shouted. 'Give us a show. We ain't bet good money for you to bilk us with a goddamn jug-head.'

Leo Grainger gripped the top rail of the corral. How the hell am I goin' to account for losin' $200, he wondered and groaned with a deep feeling of sickness. Then, to his and everyone else's amazement, the roan went into a tentative walk around the corral. It shook its head in bewilderment, swung its head from side to side as it tried to straighten its back.

The remaining crowd were restless and lusty. They would have cheered long and loud if Jude had been piled and kicked, all but killed. To them, life wasn't that cheap, but on occasion, it didn't come that dear either.

'Hey, Leo,' a man called out. 'You been grubbin' him up on the ol' mescal buttons?' The accompanying yells, although scornful, were mingled with callous hope.

Leo Grainger, still precariously perched on the fence, shook his head. 'I don't know what the duece's goin' on,' he uttered miserably. 'I never saw that roan when it didn't want to kick an' bite the moon.'

Nervously, Alice sat her own horse. She had watched every move, and was getting inquisitive. She too, had heard that the big, Roman-nosed roan was unrideable. Now it looked little more than any other tired and tender mount.

Jude tugged his sombrero down a little more firmly and drew his legs up. Then he brought them down firmly, jabbing the roan with his long-shanked spurs. The next moment the horse was in the air with its four hoofs bunched. It was arching its neck and pulling down its head, as if it wanted to see its tail under its belly. Then, humping its back it went up, and Jude hung on. But it came down with a thud and a low snuffle, flung its head and lowered its belly to the ground. Then it straightened out and twisted its great head to take a look at the saddle and Jude.

'Yeah, I'm still here, you snake-eyed devil. Try again, why don't you?' Jude rasped. Most of the women and children had gone, or been taken away by disgruntled menfolk. The few that were left, had backed off from their fence positions, were exchanging black looks with Leo Grainger.

'What say we have our own little circus, an' ride this tinhorn out o' town?' Beecher suggested.

Grainger held up a restraining hand. 'I told you, I don't know what's the matter with him. Roughin' me up won't get you your money back. An' don't forget, I'm losin' more than any o' you. Much more!'

'I ain't forgettin, Leo,' Jude called out. 'Come down here an' open the gate. Me an' Lucifer here's goin' on a constitutional.'

Grainger climbed down and with a couple of other men, dragged the gate open. Jude crow-hopped the quivering roan through the gap, held it close by the buckskin that Alice was riding.

'Why not let the lady ride him?' A man advised.

Jude gave a tight smile. 'I'm thinkin' about it,' he said.

Grainger shook his head and swore under his breath. He was of a mind not to go home. The snow-covered peaks of Shell Mountain would no doubt offer a warmer welcome.

'I kind o' like the feel o' this feller, Alice,' Jude drawled 'He's still ready to kick the lid off, but I'm goin' to try an' ride him for a spell. You want to come along?'

Alice grinned. 'Just try an' stop me,' she said.

They were going to ride the dirt track that led east from town, but almost immediately, Alice reined in.

'Wait up, Jude,' she called. 'I've just remembered my father's been tailin' me. He still is, so I'd best see what he wants.'

Jude shot her a quick look, his jaw muscles cording. 'Whatever it is, Alice, it won't be in my interest. Let's keep goin'.'

'No. If we don't wait for him here, he'll most likely follow us all the way to the foothills,' Alice reasoned.

Jude eased off the roan. 'I guess we really don't want that,' he ceded.

4

The crowd had begun to disperse but it stopped when it saw the rig fast approaching. Forbes Rickson's broad face that was sided by mutton chop whiskers was blood-pressured red. He hauled the horse back on its haunches, his indignant eyes burning as he glared first at his daughter, then Jude Linsey.

'Go home, Alice,' the man ordered through fat lips. 'Go home an' stay there.'

Alice took a deep breath and lifted her chin defiantly. 'I'm not goin' home or anywhere I don't want to, Pa,' she affirmed. 'I'm no longer a child an' I don't propose to be talked to as if I were one. An' I don't expect to be followed either.'

'You're deservin' o' whatever I decide,' he roared.

Jude dismounted and stood beside the fractious roan. His face appeared to be impassive.

With his winded rig horse needing no tether, Rickson scrambled to the ground. He reeled his short, stout body around the vehicle to where Jude was standing, and raised his whip, threateningly.

'If that girl won't take guidance from me, perhaps you will, you no-account range rat.'

'Range rat maybe, Mr Rickson, but *no account* . . . never,' Jude retorted. 'I just gone an' made myself two hundred dollars.'

'For heaven's sake, Pa, stop it,' Alice joined in. 'Have some respect for yourself, if not me.'

'Huh, the whole county probably knows where an' when respect's been lost, young lady. You've already seen to that.'

Alice dismounted, and dropped the reins of the buckskin. Her father looked from her to Jude, tightly gripped the whip with which he'd intended to lash Jude.

'Try an' touch anyone with that lash, Mr Rickson, an' I'll have to take it from you,' Jude said. As he spoke, he looked towards Alice, the uncertainty plain in his face.

It was then that the sheriff decided it was time for him to take a hand. He swaggered in and put himself between the two men. But it was under the steady bore of Jude's grey eyes that Rickson decided to lower the whip.

'That's better,' Bere said. 'I *could* call this a behaviour likely to breach the peace, an' arrest you . . . both. What's it to be?'

'This really ain't your business, Bere. Move on, or you'll be gettin' more'n the flat o' my hand in your face,' Jude responded sharply. 'Officer o' the law or not, I'm in a mood to punch right through that goddamn badge o' yours.'

'Hey. The door to one scrap closes, an' another opens up,' a man yelled from close by.

Alice was standing close to Jude as the sheriff sided with her father in recommending that she go home.

'Just shut it, Bere,' Rickson said. 'She'll do as I say without *your* meddlin'. Hitch your horse to the rig, Alice, we're goin' home *now*,' he threatened and raised his hand.

Jude was waiting for such a movement. He stepped forward and powerfully dragged the buggy whip from Rickson. The middle-aged rancher stumbled forward on to his knees.

'Goddamnit, I just got through tellin' you,' Bere snorted, and went for his holstered Colt.

But again Jude was ready. He moved swiftly for the sheriff's wrist and gripped hard. 'Pull this gun an' you'll drown in trouble,' he snapped. 'Elected law officers don't settle personal issues with bullets. Those days are gone.'

Men who knew that Jude was customarily unarmed, again began to clamour for the fight. Jude took a step back, remained a protective front for Alice.

'It sounds like a lot o' the folk in this town really ain't goin' to be satisfied until we settle up one way or another,' he challenged. Then he turned to Alice. 'Hey, Alice, don't forget the fixin's for that picnic we aim to take.'

'I won't, but meantime I'd rather stick around here,' Alice answered, sensing that Jude wanted her out of the way.

Before Jude could think of the next thing to say, everyone turned towards the town where the sound of gunfire cracked across the open ground.

'Where the hell's that comin' from?' Bere started.

Town, an' it ain't Chinee crackers,' someone yelled. 'You should be gettin' back there, Sheriff, instead o' wranglin' here with Jude.'

Forbes Rickson turned sickly pale and sweat broke across his meaty features.

The sheriff made for Rickson's rig. 'I'll use your rig,' he shouted. 'It'll save time.'

More gunfire echoed across the town's flat and featureless hinterland, then they all heard the unmistakable drumming of galloping horses. A dozen men were running back to town, but some were dragging their heels, those who were unenthusiastic in running up against unknown guns.

A group of excited, shouting boys with frantic, windmilling arms, ran from the end of town towards Eel Creek's bridge.

'The bank's been robbed,' one of them started yelling. 'The Susan Boys done it. Some of us seen 'em.'

A wave of nausea crept through Rickson and his legs nearly buckled. It sounded like his worst and timely fears had become real. Alice guessed it and moved beside him, clutched his arm in support.

Jude was watching and nodded his understanding at Alice. 'Get back in the rig, Mr. Rickson. Go with the sheriff into town,' he recommended. He picked up the man's whip and handed it to Bere, butt-first. 'Everythin' else can wait,' he said, looking him squarely in the eye.

'Yeah. Until *then*, you can help us go after the Susan Boys gang, if that's who it is,' Bere said, with a meaning that was hard to make out.

Warily, Jude shook his head, cracked what looked like a private smile. 'I don't think so, Sheriff. There's nothin' in town they could've taken that was mine.'

'Then go to hell.' With that, Bere violently lashed the rig horse, and together with Rickson, ran towards the bridge.

Alice looked sternly at Jude, then she climbed back into her saddle. 'Some time you can tell me the *real* reason,' she said coolly, and knocked the buckskin to a canter.

Leo Grainger was pulling a concerned face as he approached. 'You lost a few points with the lady there, Jude. Why *didn't* you join Bere?'

'Because I reckon he'd put a bullet in me as soon as we hit the trees.'

Leo gave a short, breathy whistle. 'Christ! You reckon?'

'Yeah, I reckon. If it was goin' to be the Susans, they'd probably be firin' from out in front, if you get my meanin'. But keep it to yourself. If you wait a

31

moment, I'll unsaddle the roan. He's back to bein'
all yours.'

'No, you've almost got the better of him. That's
more'n anyone else has. Besides, I'm in trouble
enough without trailin' the son-of-a-bitch back to the
ranch.'

Jude quickly took in Leo's offer. 'If it's your good
lady you're talkin' about, Leo, an' that little of bet,
you can keep the two hundred. I knew I could ride
him, so takin' your money wouldn't be quite right,'
he decided.

'But I've come over to settle. I've got the money
here for you.'

'I know you have, Leo, an' that's decent, but
maybe I'll take the roan in the wager's stead. That
way, some of us gets to be part pleased.'

'Yeah, OK, Jude, thanks. Now why don't we go to
town an' find out what all the fuss is about?'

'We know that already. Or do you want to bet on
it?' Jude suggested mischievously.

5

The townsfolk from the businesses close by the bank were in a state of confusion and anxiety when Jude and Leo arrived. They were mingling with those men who'd been at the horse corral, those eager to hear the story of the robbery. In the shade of one of the plaza's madrona trees, the sheriff had already been holding forth. With an extra gunbelt strapped around his waist, he was saying that he was waiting for his deputy, had enlisted three extra deputies to help form a posse.

Jude saw Alice talking to a friend. They were standing a little away from the main crowd, and Alice was holding the reins of her buckskin mare.

'There's Jude,' Milly Pease said. 'Call him over why don't you? I'd like to hear how he's got Leo Grainger's outlaw to quieten down.'

Alice sniffed. 'Weren't much of a story, Milly. An' since then he's let down not only me, but the whole town.'

'Nevertheless, I'm still interested in how he managed to break the roan.'

'Please leave it be, Milly. The only reason I'd want to see him would be to offer a white feather. He's not the man I'd reckoned him to be.'

'Alice Rickson, I declare,' Milly exclaimed. 'The sun must have got to you. Are you suggesting that he's some sort of faint heart?'

'I was there, Milly. I know what I heard and what I'm talkin' about.'

'Well, *I* don't know what it is you're talking about, Alice. Maybe those senses of yours aren't exclusive to each other,' Milly contended. 'It would take more than anything Jude Linsey says to make *me* believe he's a coward.'

Three horsemen galloped from a side street and reined up in front of the courthouse where two other saddle horses were post hitched. One of the horsemen was armed with a Winchester rifle, Cappy Rowles was carrying a long-barrelled, muzzle-loading shotgun and had a big Green River knife slung from his belt.

'Where's Pruitt?' the sheriff called out. 'Why ain't he here?'

'Don't know, boss,' Peg Fuller, the rider with the rifle said. 'But I guess he'll be here.'

'He'd goddamn better be,' Bere growled. 'I'll be ready to take up that trail in about five minutes. An' what are you doin' with that ol' fowlin' piece? I ain't

seen the like o' that for more'n ten years. Get yourself over to the office, tell Bill to hurry up, an' draw a
Winchester an' shells.'

Jude walked the roan towards an old prospect miner
whom he'd seen leading his pair of burros in from
the south end of town. 'Those fellers hightailin' it
out o' here. Which way was they headed?' he asked
him.

The man stopped, shook some dust from his
tattered outfit and spat a thin stream of dark juice. 'I
ain't seen no such fellers,' he said, without looking
up.

'Yeah you have,' Jude disagreed. 'Unless you're in
with 'em, o' course. Then I'll have to use my influ-
ence with the good sheriff, an' get you canned for a
couple o' weeks on suspicion.'

'Up to no good, were they?' the miner asked, now
giving Jude a sly look.

'Well, they robbed the bank,' Jude offered wryly.

The miner spluttered out some laughter. He
nodded in the direction of Shell Mountain. 'Four of
'em, an' they'll soon be into the timber.'

'Then that'll be a real dangerous place to be,' Jude
said, and waved a hand as he walked back to the
plaza.

'What's the matter with that sheriff?' Leo Grainger
asked. 'Why don't he go after 'em? If they *are* the
Susan Boys, they'll have someone with 'em who
knows every hole an' dog hollow along the line.'

35

'You're right, Leo. An' it ain't goin' to be *our* sheriff who catches 'em if he leaves it much longer.'

'Why don't *you* go find 'em, Jude?' Aldo Beecher said as he walked up.

'Yeah, you know where they're likely to make for better than any man hereabouts,' another man pointed out.

'I ain't lost any bank robbers,' Jude answered them.

'I don't suppose your pa would see the funny side o' that, Jude. An' that ain't personal . . . just a goddamn fact,' Leo said.

Jude ground his teeth as he pictured his father refusing him the loan of $200. 'I can't answer for my father,' he shrugged. 'If he's that concerned, perhaps he could pay someone to bring 'em in. Say, two hundred dollars?' he added dispassionately.

Beecher shook his head, shuffled his feet uncomfortably as he looked past Jude. Then the men moved away as if they suddenly wanted to break the association. A moment later, Jude turned when he felt a hand on his shoulder.

'Two hundred dollars ain't a high price for bringin' in a bunch o' stick-up thug killers. You sure are a curiously baked brick, aren't you, Son?' Noel Linsey growled.

Jude met his father's eyes. 'Is there some part o' my way of thinkin' you don't like?' he responded.

'It's bein' said that you refused to go along with the sheriff's posse,' Linsey stated after a moment's thought. 'Is that somethin' you got an answer for, too?'

'Yeah. I've just got through sayin' that it ain't *me* who's lost out.'

'What *I* lose, you do too, Son. So why not rethink your decision about joinin' the posse?' was Linsey's more barbed approach.

'I already have, Pa. If I'm goin' into the mountains, it'll be to fish for steelheads.'

The sheriff and his posse of deputy Hank Bosun and the three sworn-in members, galloped off in a great cloud of stirred-up dust. They were headed for Shell Mountain while Jude made his way to the Blue Coop saloon.

'I'm returnin' that two hundred,' Jude said, as he laid the twenty-dollar coins on the bar in front of Corbett Welt. 'An' thank you. The ol' roan weren't as hard to stay on as I thought he'd be.'

'Wasn't he just,' said the saloon owner, looking keenly at Jude. 'Well, I reckon that horse is every bit as treacherous as you know it to be. So I reckon there's somethin' else went on for you to make that ride.'

'But if only we knew *what*,' Jude said enigmatically.

'Yeah, an' there's somethin' behind why you refused to ride along with the sheriff's posse, too. I get to learn a lot just by watchin', Jude.'

'Well, a good man don't need watchin' an' a bad one usually ain't worth it. My pa told me that,

Corbett,' Jude retorted, tapped a finger along the side of his nose.

'I reckon it's somethin' to do with Alice Rickson,' Welt continued, unabashed.

'You just continue with your reckonin', Corbett. Now, if you don't mind, I got a horse still to ride.'

Welt moved over to the doors of the saloon, held up a hand to stop their swing after Jude had stepped into the street. 'He could be holdin' an ace high, an' you'd think it was a runnin' flush,' he muttered with a wry smile. A few moments later, he thought it strange that the two young women he saw walk past Jude should turn their heads away quite so obviously. He couldn't see Jude's face, but he reckoned there'd be some sort of surprise working across it. Yeah, there's something going on there, he thought. Perhaps young Jude *is* holding the flush.

6

From the excitement directly following the bank robbery, the situation became one of doubt and fear. Many men and women had deposited small savings in the bank, in addition to the comparatively large accounts of Noel Linsey and Forbes Rickson.

The damage created by the Susan Boys gang in towns along the line of the Great Northern Rail Road had been of limited interest in Spooner's Drift. But now that had changed. Twenty thousand dollars or thereabouts had been taken from the bank – almost all the cash that had been held there.

Could Ogden Sayler, the owner of the bank, find capital to reopen? was one of the first major concerns among the account holders.

'You lose much?' Aldo Beecher was asking.

'No. Most o' my money's on the hoof. Until them Susans take up rustlin' I'll be OK,' one of those with a small ranch responded.

'Yeah, it's an ill wind, eh! But a bank with no

dollars ain't much use to man nor beast. If anyone had ever thought of stoppin' off at Red Bluff an' takin' a buggy ride out this way, they won't *now* . . . except maybe to have a laugh,' Beecher continued drolly.

There was already a meeting taking place in the courthouse. It was urgently convened to decide upon the reward that was to be offered for the capture of the Susan Boys gang, dead or alive. Before he'd left with his posse, Ingram Bere had telegraphed sheriffs' offices along the railroad line, advising them of the raid.

'Maybe Sheriff Bere *can* bring down them robbers,' the rancher remarked.

'He'll have trouble,' Beecher growled. 'From what I heard, those robbers show up, rob the bank or train an' then skedaddle, shootin' anybody who gets in their way. They leave tracks for five or ten miles, then disappear into thin air, until the next time.'

'Well if you want my opinion,' put in a man who'd little to say up to that point, 'there's one feller who could at least find 'em. Someone who knows the features o' the land.'

'If you're talkin' o' Jude Linsey, he wouldn't even ride with the posse when the sheriff asked him,' said Franklin Teller who ran the livery stable. 'Do you know where he is right now? Why, foolin' around with that devil roan. With his poor ol' father havin' lost just about everythin' it's hard to tell which one's the son-of-a-bitch.'

'Ah, Jude's all right,' Beecher insisted. 'There ain't no tellin' what's goin' on in the young feller's head. But he must have some good reason for what he's doin'.'

'Yeah, that's what I'm sayin',' Teller said. 'I give it some thought, an' wondered if he was in cahoots with the Susans.'

Leo Grainger gave a hollow laugh. 'You been mixin' with dumb animals for too long, Teller,' he said derisively. Then he went to his buggy, climbed aboard and drove from town in the direction of his ranch.

But some men remained and continued to listen.

'O' course Linsey wouldn't join no posse,' Teller warmed to his presumption. 'If there's a hand that's feedin' him, he ain't goin' to bite it, is he? I know Grainger says he wouldn't take the two hundred he won off him, but we only got his word.'

The few scattered houses on the southerly outskirts of the town were almost deserted. Their owners were in town, nervous with the excitement caused by the bank robbery. As Jude Linsey walked past, he chewed his lip, was saddened at the way Alice Rickson had acted towards him.

'So have the good sheriff if you want him,' he muttered, moments later. 'I'll wager he'll turn in to a prince after his first kiss.'

Well beyond the last house, almost into the timber, Jude reset the saddle. He rubbed the roan's neck, talked quiet and slow for a minute or two.

'Now I'm goin' to ride you proper,' he said, as he laid his left hand on the saddle horn. 'I know we done it once, but saddle broke's one thing . . . saddle *friendly's* another.'

The roan turned its head and boggled its eyes. Then Jude was in the saddle, his right foot shooting the stirrup. Immediately the roan humped its back and lowered its head. Jude let the reins slip through his left hand, and he stretched his legs. Then he bent his knees and jounced back into the saddle before the roan could go into the air. As the horse hit the ground again it bowed its back and shuddered.

Jude prodded with the spurs. 'Whoever told you you were a buck jumper?' he said. 'Come on, let's do some real learnin'.'

The roan went into the air, came down grunting and shaking. It went up again and again. Then it stopped and lowered its head. Jude nudged its flanks, and holding its head to one side, it began to walk huffily, ears twitching. As Jude's spurs pricked again, it wheeled and went into the air once more. As it landed, Jude felt a jerk and a stab of pain in his spine.

'Yeah, that's more like it, feller. Takes a little mean-ness to get you goin', but no more spurs eh?'

The roan did seem to be through with its bucking. It walked, then went into a slow trot, and Jude could-n't get it to go into the air again. At last it had begun to understand who was boss.

'See, it makes sense to get friendly. Who'd ever

have thought it – a horse with brains.'

Jude was so engrossed in his exchanges with the roan, that he didn't turn to greet the rider who had approached through a break in the timber. The man was bow-backed in the saddle and the mule was elderly, but it wore the scut of a white rabbit stitched into the middle of its brow-band.

The salty old rider's head was covered by a coon cap, and a shock of white hair hung down to his buckskin-clad shoulders. He reined the mule up, and his brown face broke into a deep wrinkly smile.

'Well, what we got here?' he wheezed, snaking bridle reins through his bony fingers. 'Has that roan been jimson-weeded?'

'No. It's just natural born spite,' Jude said, as he pulled the roan down. 'It's good to see you, Pipestone.'

'Yeah, surprised as well, with me stealin' up on you like that.'

'You didn't steal up on me. From aways back, I saw jays risin' from the tops o' them pines.'

'Ha,' the old man chortled. 'He's the outlaw that Leo Grainger's been tryin' to sell, ain't he? You gone an' bought him?'

'Kind of, yeah. What do you think?'

Pipestone eyed the horse. 'Mules show me respect,' he said. 'I reckon it would be the other way round with him.'

'You don't like him then?'

'That ain't what I said,' Pipestone chided.

Jude dismounted and dropped the reins. The roan tried to sidle away until it felt the drag on its nose, then it stopped. It shook, swung back its head and bit savagely at one front corner of the saddle skirt.

'You sure he ain't got a burr under there somewhere?' Pipestone remarked. 'A tick maybe?'

Jude shook his head. 'Yeah, I'm sure,' he said thoughtfully. 'He just wants back to the open range.'

With unexpected agility, Pipestone dismounted. His mule dropped its head for an opportune nap, and the old man sat down cross-legged in the shelter of its belly.

'I got me a thirst . . . was on my way to town for a liquor jug,' he said. 'What's the news?'

Jude explained briefly about the bank robbery. 'O' course with the places you get to frequent, I don't know whether that's news to you or not,' he added.

'Well, from what I heard, it sounds like the Susans all right. There's two of 'em, Dooley an' Boot, an' two others that ain't family. An' you're supposin' they took to the mountain?'

Jude nodded. 'Yeah, where else? There's a million places to lose yourself between here an' the track, or here an' the ocean. Four fellers could be no more'n ten feet away from you in that timber, an' you'd never know.'

'I would,' Pipestone asserted with a whiskery grin. 'I also heard that every time they rob somethin' or somebody along the line, they never once went into the timber. So my guess is they're ridin' the Bull Chop, most likely double back north or south along it.'

'Thanks. I'll bear that in mind.'

'You do, an' keep your eyes peeled. Won't do any harm to keep your hand on the stock of a saddle gun either. You don't want anyone creepin' up on you, again,' Pipestone sniggered.

'Now I got me a real Sunday horse, I'll try ridin' him back into town,' Jude said with dry humour. 'Perhaps we can stand each other somethin' to cut the dust.'

7

Overlooking the town of Spooner's Drift, the Linsey home stood close to the fringe of redwood and pine. The house was unique because it was painted white, was of two storeys and circled by a dozen black oaks. Back of it was the housemaid's lodge, a small barn and a carriage house large enough for the buggy and the family surrey.

It was approaching full dark when Jude rode into the back yard. He was on the roan that wasn't yet eager to have anything to do with a corral or stable building. Back in the timber a fox barked; from the town a scavenger dog answered and the roan flicked its ears.

After unsaddling and putting his gear in its usual place, Jude led the roan to a small, but solid-built corral. He tied its head close down to a post and, working carefully, he hobbled the animal. 'You won't go jumpin' any o' these fences,' he said, and patted the roan's neck.

A few minutes later he tossed over a forkload of hay, and then brought over a can of oats, shoved them under the fence near the hay. He filled a pail with water, opened the gate and set it inside. 'Get freshed up, boy. We got somewhere to go. People an' places to see.'

For a while, Jude stood with his arms folded across the top of the fence. As the roan tentatively snatched at a mouthful of hay, his mind got to wandering. Until this afternoon he hadn't looked upon life as a very special or serious affair. He hadn't the need to. But now, and all of a sudden, he'd started to think otherwise. Perhaps it was the breaking of the roan, the settling in to something more customary and thorough.

His father had lost a small fortune, and maybe he should start by giving *that* some real thought; thoughts on how to get it back. But that wouldn't include any help for Forbes Rickson, he told himself. The only good thing to come out of that would be for the man's daughter to come and say, sorry and thank you.

Then his thoughts turned to Pipestone, and what the old trapper had meant by him needing to keep his eyes peeled if he was to go into the big timber. And he was to go armed. Nevertheless, Jude might take a ride up to the head o' the creek. Beyond that, it was mostly virgin land, other than Pipestone's spore and a few old Indian bones.

'But first I got me an appointment in town, an' the

less *they* know about *any* o' this, the better,' he muttered, referring to his mother and father. Then he turned, tensed, as a wedge of light suddenly broke from the house when the scullery door opened.

Rachel Fletcher, the Linsey household's maid, had been watching silently from the small window in the scullery.

'I don't suppose you'll be comin' in?' she asked quietly, as she approached Jude from across the yard. 'There's cold cuts, bread an' butter.'

'Thanks, Rachel, but no. An' don't you go sayin' anythin' about where I'm gone,' he said.

'Well, I don't *know*, do I? But I can guess it's got somethin' to do with Sheriff Bere, an' that Susan gang. Just make sure you don't go into town, armed. You hear me?'

'It matters to you, does it, Rachel, whether I do or not?' he answered back, boorishly.

'Every family's got a goddess of mercy, Jude. Just leave your gun behind,' she said unhappily and turned back to the house.

An hour later, Jude looked around him at the lamps that shed illumination in and out of the town's small stores and businesses. In the plaza, he might, at some other time, have stopped to talk with some of the townsfolk. But this night, because he had an inkling of the nature of their conversation, he walked on.

Where a small crowd had gathered in front of the bank, Jude dismounted. He could see that several men, including his father, were inside. The agitated voices immediately dropped to a suspicious murmur, and someone made an obvious derogatory remark. Another opinion followed with a comment about Jude's reluctance to join the sheriff's posse.

'Not even to help his own pa,' someone else sneered.

'Is one o' you suggestin' I'm a yellow-belly?' Jude directed his question towards the faceless voice. 'If you are, at least say it to my face.'

'It ain't just *one* of us,' the man known as Turkel said. 'Take a look around you, Linsey.'

Three other men were ready for the confrontation and they shouldered their way forward. The crowd almost instantly thinned, as those worried at the possibility of gun or knife play turned fearful.

'Great goddamn odds,' Jude muttered, as he went for the first of the advancing men, raising the cold sliver of a smile at the challenger. 'It's goin' to be you, feller,' he said, and swung a bone-hard fist into the man's aggressive features.

With a cracked and bloodied nose, the man staggered back. He was going to fall between his two colleagues, but both men instinctively grabbed an arm and held him on his feet. They hadn't time to make another move before Jude took a couple of steps forward and gave each one a great pounding blow to the belly.

Jude swung round to face Turkel, who was staring at the three men who'd crumpled to the ground.

'This don't mean I ain't whatever you're thinkin', friend. But I reckon it's put a stop to you comin' forward an' sayin' so.' Jude rubbed his knuckles, half wished Turkel would want his own fight.

'Why was half the town bein' entertained at the horse corral this afternoon while the bank was bein' robbed?' Turkel demanded. 'How'd you explain that?'

'Yeah, I had nineteen dollars in there,' one of the townsmen went along.

'I had more'n forty,' growled another. 'I can't afford to lose that.'

'If there is an explanation, I don't know what it is,' Jude answered. 'But you ain't the only losers. My pa lost plenty, an' so did his company, you all know that. An' I know that if nineteen dollars is all you got, that's plenty, too. But if anyone mouths off that I had anythin' to do with the robbery, I'll take somethin' from 'em they really can't afford to lose. That, I promise.'

Ogden Sayler walked over from the bank. 'I come to let you all know that we're conferrin' to find the best way to help *all* the bank's depositors,' he said, looking around him. 'What we don't need right now is more trouble. It don't help.'

'What we don't need is trouble brought about by Jude Linsey,' the man who'd lost more than forty dollars said.

'That sounds to me like you're suggestin' my boy's in cahoots,' Noel Linsey shouted out from the boardwalk. Quite unexpectedly, he grabbed a rifle from one of the two men who'd been guarding the doors of the bank and swung it threateningly out in front of him.

Jude cursed. He knew his father's capacity for anger, but didn't always appreciate the incitement. He was moving to intervene, when Corbett Welt came crashing out through the doors of his Blue Coop saloon.

'You want any help, boy?' he shouted excitedly. 'By God, there's one thing I won't stand aside for, an' that's an unfair scrap. You hold 'em up, Jude, an' I'll dispatch 'em for you. It's what we got given fists for.'

Jude was looking to see whether Welt had anyone particular in mind, when a neighbour of Leo Grainger's came rushing up the street from the direction of the livery stable.

'We got more trouble,' he yelled. 'Ol' Pipestone's threatening to skin Frank Teller. He'll have sawn right through his neck if someone don't get to him soon. I seen his face an' he means it.'

8

Jude, fearing that the old mountain man was committing some sort of gory murder, made it fast to the livery barn. He turned through the wide double-doors, stopped and spread his arms. 'You stayed well behind on the way here, now keep it that way,' he rasped as a few followers-on, pressed up for a look.

In the middle of the stinking, dirt floor, Franklin Teller lay very still. Astride him was Pipestone, pinning the liveryman down with his knees. He was cackling and brandishing his skinning knife as if he was whetting the blade in the heavy, fetid air. As he swept the long thin blade towards the man's nose, Teller whimpered, tried desperately to turn his face to the ground.

'Shut whinin', or I'll draw this meat slicer across your throat. Let's all hear what you been sayin' about Jude Linsey.'

'Get off me. I was only sayin' . . . repeatin' what I heard,' Teller snuffled.

The tip of Pipestone's knife pierced the hard-packed dirt an inch from Teller's ear. He jerked it free, swung it in a fast arc above the man's face to within an inch of his other ear. 'Next time, one o' these fat ol' lugs comes off like a wedge o' blood puddin'. Now, as the man himself's standin' right here, tell us *who* an' *what* was said about him.'

'He's had enough, Pipe,' Jude said, stepping forward. 'He would've told you by now if he knew anythin'. Go on, let him up.'

The old trapper jerked his head about and grinned. 'He's sayin' it weren't *him* startin' any big windy, but I reckon it was. I'd have got it out o' him soon enough, no need for you to get involved, son. I would've let you know what's what.'

Teller scrabbled frantically to his knees. Then he stood muttering and grimacing, swaying from side to side, his frightened eyes held to the glittering blade of Pipestone's knife. 'It weren't me,' he shrieked.

'Hey, Pipestone,' a man called out as he moved in through the doors of the barn. 'If this lizard tail's claimin' Jude Linsey's in cahoots with them bank robbers, then he more'n likely ain't. You thought o' that?'

'Yeah, ain't *that* the truth,' someone else said, after everyone had thought for a moment. 'Teller really is the damnest liar ever to drag his sorry ass through these parts. Let's string him up for a little ol' choke.'

'No,' Teller screeched. The man was so scared, he was rooted to the spot. Only his jaw was working. 'I was jus' fool enough to repeat what I heard. I'll swear it on a stack o' Bibles.'

'Yeah, the one's you'll be steppin' off,' Pipestone grunted.

Jude shook his head with displeasure and indifference. 'Let's go get a couple o' them dust cutters we owe ourselves,' he suggested. 'He really ain't done me any more harm than's been done already.'

'Maybe so. An' maybe I'll call in an' see him later,' Pipestone threatened.

In his office back of the stable, Franklin Teller didn't light his lamp. He fumbled about for a bottle and sat on the edge of his threadbare couch to take a gulping swallow.

'I ain't sleepin' up on this,' he vowed. 'I if do, that goddamned bear's ass Pipestone'll come back to stick me.' Teller grabbed a cushion and, with the bottle, he rolled to the floor and crawled beneath the couch. He lay on his back, sucked on the remaining whiskey dregs and within ten minutes was away in a dead-beat sleep.

It was less than an hour on, but Teller realized he wasn't dreaming about the horse that was tramping around the hitching floor. It was there, and its handler was calling his name.

'Who the hell's makin' all that fuss? Is that *you* come back, Pipestone?' Teller wanted to know as he edged himself towards the light.

'Christ, I ain't seen much worse crawl from under

a horse turd,' Ingram Bere grated. 'Come on out an'
take care o' my horse.'

Teller scrambled to his feet, pulled at his pants
and scratched his head. 'You got them bank robbers
with you, Sheriff?' he asked abstractedly.

'No, I ain't got no goddamn robbers,' Bere
growled back. 'All I got's a bad headache an' a lot o'
sore bones. I need some sleep, an' my horse taken
care of.'

Teller sat down on the edge of his makeshift bed.
'What happened then?'

'Look, I want a few hours on that bug pit o' yours.
I'll give you five dollars for the use of it, an' to keep
your mouth shut.'

'Help if I knew what for,' Teller suggested foxily.

'We got bushwhacked up in the timber. I think
they got Saul Pruitt. We got split up, so maybe Fuller
an' Rowles got back. I don't know. I don't even know
what happened to my own goddamn deputy. I got to
get some sleep. Now, shut it, Teller. Remember you
been warned to keep quiet, an' I'm the law.'

When Jude and Pipestone went into the Blue Coop
saloon, Corbett Welt was back of the bar. There were
a few drinkers in front of it and, almost impercepti-
bly, they moved away.

'You know what I want, Corbett,' the old hunter
grunted. 'An' I ain't in a waitin' frame o' mind.'

'I'll have a beer,' Jude said, half turned when the
group of men walked off, noisily pushed open the

batwings and disappeared into the street.

'Huh, somethin' I said?' Pipestone asked, with a tight little grin as he filled his glass to brimming.

'More'n likely, somethin *they* was sayin',' one of two men who were sitting at a nearby table said.

Jude turned to look at them, nodded at the man's summing up. 'You two fellers have a drink?' he offered.

'Yeah, why not? We ain't got no quarrel,' the man, who's name was Monte Kinnan, said.

'Hey, listen, Jude,' Welt said, leaning forward after Jude had handed over the topped up glasses. 'What are the chances o' Bere bringin' in the Susan Boys? Do you reckon he can prise 'em out o' that mountain timber?'

'Hee hee. You got more chance o' gettin' manure from a younker's rockin' horse,' Pipestone butted in.

They laughed, and Kinnan's friend raised his glass. 'Hey, Pipestone,' he said. 'There's talk that that old flea-bag mule outside is even older than you.'

'There's nothin' older'n me, mister. 'Cept your jokes maybe.'

Jude took a pull on his beer to finish it, and placed the empty glass meditatively on the counter. 'I'm goin' now,' he said. 'I'm goin' to call in on that pa o' mine. You just promise me one thing, Pipe.'

'Promises are like pie crusts, young feller . . . made to be broken.'

'Humour me then,' Jude asked. 'Stay away from the livery stable an' Frank Teller.'

The two guards were still in front of the bank when Jude approached. He asked Max, who was Monte Kinnan's brother, if it was OK for him to go in.

'Sure. There ain't nothin' o' much value left,' he said with an ironic grin.

The interior of the bank was lit by clusters of bracket lamps. Jude knocked on the polished door marked PRIVATE, waited until it was opened by Ogden Sayler.

'Ah, you'll be wantin' to see your pa,' the bank's proprietor said.

'Come on in, Jude,' his father called out. 'You'll have met most o' these men.'

Jude went into the large office and nodded at the handful of stockholders.

'Hello. Do you know where Alice is?' Forbes Rickson asked directly.

'No. An' don't rightly know that I should,' Jude answered just as stiffly. 'Are you comin' home?' he said, addressing himself to his father.

'Yeah, why not. I'm tired, an' it's too late for much else this night.'

'Sorry, feller. You really are one irate son-of-a-bitch, ain't you?' Jude had said, in tying his anxious roan to the back of his father's buggy. 'I know you ain't *ever* goin' to get genuine saddle happy.'

The two men were halfway back to the ranch, before Noel Linsey spoke. 'Have you an' Alice had some sort o' ruckus?' he asked.

'Yeah, a Rickson ruckus,' Jude replied. 'She's mad 'cause I decided not to ride with the sheriff. That's the fat o' the reason. Why?'

'Nothin' much. Maybe the name Rickson never got me kicked off good. She wouldn't be thinkin' what some o' those other considerate folk are thinkin', would she?'

'I don't know what it is they're thinkin,' Jude replied, his voice with an antagonistic edge. 'She's a disappointment though . . . not the girl I thought she was if she's got me down as one o' Dooley Susan's boys.'

'Did you work out your losses?' Jude asked, a few awkward and meaningful minutes later.

'Yeah, I did. It's gettin' on for ten thousand. An' it's money we ain't likely to get back.'

Jude sucked air through his teeth. 'Jeez, that's more'n chick feed. How about the bank?'

'Sacramento will cash cover any out o' town cheques, an' they'll open up a workin' float. Ogden promises business within a couple o' weeks.'

The two men then rode in silence until the circle of darkly silhouetted black oaks came into view.

'That'll be Rachel, waitin' up,' Noel Linsey said, seeing the yellow flicker of house lights ahead of them. 'But if it's your ma, Jude, don't mention the loss. It's made me feel sick to the stomach; heaven knows what it'll do to *her*.'

9

As Teller went about his work at the stable, he kept a wary eye out for Pipestone. After his late-night confrontation with the ornery mountain man, and then an early morning one with Ingram Bere, he was suffering, in need of his customary 'get-going' whiskey. Beside that, he was fit to bust with the news of Bere's return to town. His avowed silence on the matter was about as fickle as fortune.

'I'll wager Bere got some of them robbers,' he muttered to himself. 'He's just bein' a mite secretive, so's he can smoke out the others, that's what.'

The sun was on the rise and he was considerin' the Blue Coop, when he it occurred to him that the region in between might bear the mark of old Pipestone. But he wasn't actually that afraid, not enough to run and hide. They'd known each other too long to do anything life threatening. Most of their stuff was harsh and for their own distraction.

'I know what I'll do,' he decided. 'I'll take me a pitchfork along. The trouble with shooters is, they have a habit of going off. An' that old goat never goes round with anything more'n his skinner when he's in town.'

Teller got the pitchfork with its long sharp tines, albeit rusted from too little use. 'Can't carry it into the Coop . . . better leave it outside,' he went on with his low utterances. 'There's some have a mount needs hitchin', I got me a haysticker.'

He'd already made a practice thrust when he saw that Pipestone himself had appeared, was silently standing in the barn's doorway.

'Christ, Pipe, you scare the pants off me standin' there like that,' he gasped. 'Don't go comin' in, or this fork's headin' for your goddamn bread wallet.'

'Hah, what's the matter with you, Frank? You look like someone scared o' their own shadow,' Pipestone wheedled.

'I'm tellin' you, Pipe. Don't get me mad.'

'I only came to offer you a drink. Ol' friends shouldn't go to sleep on a disagreement, or wake on one. What d'you say?'

'Put whatever you got on the floor, an' move away,' Teller commanded.

Pipestone withdrew a flat-shaped bottle of mescal from deep within his skin rags. He placed it on the ground in front of him and took a step back. 'There, Frank. Your daybreak juice,' he gestured.

Teller, keeping the pitchfork in one hand, moved

forward cautiously. 'What you playin' at?' he asked nervously.

'Nothin'. I'm nowhere near the goddamn stuff. I know'd you wouldn't trust me to hand it to you.'

Teller moved forward. In his eagerness for the liquor, and bending to lift the bottle with his left hand, he let the fork drop from his right. He quickly tried to retrieve it, and in doing so, dropped the bottle.

'You ought to be an entertainer, Frank,' Pipestone guffawed. 'That's a real funny routine.'

Teller cursed and made another grab for the bottle. He thumbed out the cork and took a great, sucking draught.

'Hey, it ain't *all* for you,' Pipestone yelled. 'I paid good money.'

'You still bent on slicin' me, Pipe? Like you were last night?'

'That was just funnin', Frank. The sentiment of what I was sayin' ain't changed much, I guess, but I'd never harm a hair o' your head, an' you know it.'

Teller spat into the dust and sniffed. 'Yeah, says you.'

'Let's take a pew,' Pipestone suggested. The two men sat on a hay bale and passed the bottle between them for ten minutes, until there was nothing left. But it was another ten before Teller had divulged all he had to know about Ingram Bere's return to town.

'So, he's here? Right here?' Pipestone asked, low and secretive.

'Yeah, an' snufflin' like a new born. What do you reckon on that?' Teller offered.

'I don't know. If that's what he's sayin', it sure *sounds* like a big windy, but which way's it blowin'? It's a real curious situation, Frank.'

'Yeah sure is, Pipe. An' I'd like to know who it was started the hogwash about Jude bein' abed with them Susans.'

'It really weren't you then, Frank?'

'No, it weren't me. I already told you, I just passed it on. I don't even mind the boy. Anyone who prefers fishin' to countin' dollars, can't be all bad. You know that.'

'I sure do. That's where I'd known him from – hangin' trout, high along Eel Creek.' Pipestone eased himself up from the hay bale. 'So, you take good care o' my mule, Frank. Give her hay, an' as much oats as she wants.'

'As soon as I've put away me breakfast,' Teller said. 'An' I'll let you know what it was that fetched our brave sheriff back.'

'Yeah, well, it saves me tryin' to do it. Did I ever tell you about a breakfast I once had up in the timber country?' Pipestone asked.

'No you never did. What was it?'

'A quart o' pine top, a fried slab o' blackjack steer, an' a loan o' the wood hawk's dog.'

'Huh? What was the dog for?'

'He ate the goddamn meat,' Pipestone cackled, walked from the barn in the midst of a racking cough.

As soon as the old mountain man was out of sight, Teller sluiced himself in the horse trough. Spluttering, and with water still dribbling from the tips of his whiskers, he looked out the stable door to see Milly Pease standing there watching him.

'I've seen sparrows in the dust make less fuss, Mr Teller,' she said, with a broad smile. 'Perhaps you can tell me about Sheriff Bere's whereabouts. I'm thinkin' you'd be one of the first to know.'

Teller sniffed importantly, pulled on his dirt-splattered hat and stepped outside of the barn. 'Well now,' he started, 'if I *do*, would it be worth a kiss from a pretty lady?'

'Why of course,' Milly said, and fluttered an appealing eyelid.

'You know what they say about him who fights an' runs away? Well, he's back. But if he knows I told you. . . .'

'I won't tell,' Milly put in. 'I'll just have to wait awhile.'

'Worth that kiss?' Teller asked smarmily.

Milly's smile dropped a fraction. 'Mr Teller, you really are the town's Merry-Andrew. I'd rather be seen steppin' out with ol' Pipestone's mule you've got back there.' The smile broadened again, and Milly turned on her heel and walked briskly away.

'Huh, that's a real picky lady,' Teller muttered as the girl hurried away. 'This bein' the cleanest I been since last Sunday, it's her loss.'

10

Rachel Fletcher walked up to Jude who was standing outside of the corral. He was watching the roan, glistening dark against the colour of the rising sun.

'Have you seen 'em?' the Linseys' maid asked.

'Oh yeah, I've seen 'em. An' it looks like they're comin' down from big timber.'

'The posse, do you think?'

'Yeah, two of 'em anyway. It's Cappy Rowles, an' I think the other one's Peg Fuller. You better go get some coffee an' stuff, Rachel. From the way they're ridin', they ain't just started out.'

Jude walked out to meet the two riders who were slumped in their saddles. Both of them were gaunt-featured and carried dust-caked stubbly beards.

'Welcome, fellers. You run into trouble?' Jude asked, as he reached for the bridle of Fuller's horse. 'You look like you're about to take the quick route to ground.'

'I don't know how the hell I got this far,' Fuller grunted.

'It was the Susans,' Rowles said. 'We ran right into 'em late yesterday. They were lyin' for us up near to the goddamn snowline.'

'Where's Bere?' Jude wanted to know.

'I don't know,' Rowles replied despairingly. 'We had to turn and scatter.'

'Did you manage any return fire?'

'Yeah, some. There weren't much time for anythin' considered, Jude. All we thought about was gettin' out o' range. Ain't you heard anythin' from Bere? He was tramplin' brush like a grizzly last time we saw him.'

'No, he ain't been seen down here. Maybe they shot him,' Jude said, with a shake of his head. He was thinking that if it had been him up there, Bere would somehow have managed to put a bullet in him, if not in the Susan Boys.

'Serve him right if he was,' Fuller mumbled, as though matching Jude's thoughts. 'It was *him* led us into the trap.'

'An' *I* wouldn't lose any sleep over it,' Rowles agreed. 'The man weren't goin' to listen to us.'

Jude managed a wry smile. 'No need for that sort o' talk, boys. He is our sheriff after all ... or was. Come on into the house,' he invited. 'Rachel's makin' coffee. She'll probably stir it with forty-rod to get you into town.'

Jude walked with Fuller's horse, and Rowles

nodded his appreciation and followed. Fuller was badly fatigued and slipped stiffly to the ground near the scullery door. 'I've had it with posse ridin',' Jude,' he said. 'Scramblin' up an' down mountains day an' night ain't my idea of earnin' an extra dollar. An' gettin' shot at don't make it any better. But you already got your own ideas on that score, eh, Jude?' he added, a touch contrarily.

Jude didn't respond to the insinuation. 'Yeah, that's right, Peg,' he answered flatly 'But we'll soon have you fixed up.'

Rachel came back on to the scullery porch then to see what was happening. 'Did you have a fight with the Susan Boys?' she asked of the two posse men. 'Did you shoot any of 'em? Were any of 'em killed?'

To Jude, it seemed that Rachel's questions were curiously desperate, more than a likely interest. 'They don't know that, Rachel. But probably not,' he said.

'We never even got to scratch 'em,' Rowles answered. 'Take some sweet fixin's up to 'em, if you're concerned for their welfare,' he added tartly.

'Yeah, Rachel, what's all that about?' Jude asked. 'They ain't exactly family. Let's just get these fellers cleaned up an' somethin' inside of 'em.'

'Yes, I'm sorry, Jude. Cleaned up . . . food, yes,' Rachel said, and went to get the food and drink ready.

A half-hour later, after they'd eaten, Jude was just saying he'd go into town with the two men, when

Pipestone arrived.

'I come to see you, Jude. There's someone I think you should be seein' back in town,' he said with understated concern. 'He came in early this mornin', an' I thought you'd want to know.'

'OK, I'll take the surrey in. These two ain't fit to ride another mile,' Jude replied.

'Just *who* are you talkin' about?' Rachel asked. Her concern was still evident, and her dark features had visibly paled. 'Jude don't want to go to meetin' someone without knowin' who it is. Not at this time he don't. Who is it?'

'Our brave sheriff, Ingram Bere. I ain't seen 'im personal, but Frank Teller says he rode in at first light. He's over at the livery right now . . . wants it kept quiet, apparently.'

'Oh does he? Well, wantin' ain't always what you get,' Jude said with a friendly wink for Rachel.

11

Cappy Rowles and Peg Fuller thanked Rachel for the fare. 'We weren't expectin' it. Maybe we can call in next time we're in a similar fix,' Rowles said, as he dragged his hat back on to his head.

'I'm doubtin' there'll be a next time,' Fuller added sternly. 'I ain't goin' to be fooled twice.'

An hour later, the two erstwhile posse men were making their way down First Street, with Jude and Pipestone.

'You reckon Bere chickened out, 'cause of what might happen if you ran into the Susans?' Jude said, turning to Rowles who was sitting alongside him.

'Yeah, that's about the meat of it,' Rowles growled. 'He didn't have the guts to stay an' fight. Goddamnit, we could've fought them Susans. That's what we went up there for. An' I think maybe we could've saved Saul Pruitt from gettin' shot. I'm sure lookin' forward to seein' Sheriff Bere again.'

Pipestone leaned across into the surrey, from his

mule. 'Are you sure Pruitt was killed? You saw it?' he wanted to know.

'Well, I don't know if I saw him dead. But I saw him shot from the saddle. When he hit the ground, his horse kicked him in the head. What do *you* think?'

Outside of the Blue Coop saloon, a small crowd was milling. They'd learned from Franklin Teller of the sheriff's return to town, that a fruitless search for him had already been made.

'You got some maw on you, Teller, an' I wouldn't trust anythin' that comes out of it,' Fuller carped.

Travis Pearl who ran one of the town's two lodging-houses, said there was the possibility that the sheriff had gone somewhere else to sleep. 'I been about since sun-up, an' it's only dust been lyin' in his rooms,' he said.

Some wit-snapper agreed. He suggested that now Jude Linsey had been publicly given his marching orders, they all go and look under Alice Rickson's cot. The man immediately caught Jude's icy glare, and there was little more than a few doubtful smiles.

'It's Bere's horse in the stable. An' his traps,' Teller claimed. 'An' it's the same mount he rode out on.'

'What were you sayin' about his rifle?' Pearl asked.

'It was the carbine. He had it looped to his saddle horn when he left town. It wasn't there when he came back. I'd'a noticed.'

'He kept a spare saddle horse in Vaughan's home pasture,' Cappy Rowles said. 'Perhaps someone ought to go take a look.'

'No need,' Vaughan Mallit said, suddenly pushing forward. 'It's gone. That, an' the spare saddle an' bridle. An' it didn't kick no fences down either . . . even closed the darned gate after it.'

'Sure sounds like he's puttin' ground between him and Spooner's Drift. It wouldn't surprise me if he's gone to join up with them Susans,' Pipestone suggested.

'Makes a lot o' sense, I suppose,' Mallit said without too much thought. 'Good cover too, bein' a respected an' elected town sheriff an' all.'

'Slow down, fellers,' Pearl objected. 'What if he rode in here dead beat, but it was just to get a fresh horse. He had nowhere else to go. Now he's already back chasin' them bank robbers again. Ain't that just as likely?'

'Yeah, 'course it is,' Peg Fuller said with a tired and disdainful laugh. 'Why is it we never thought o' that?'

'Perhaps it's because we're the ones who saw him skedaddle as fast as his horse would take him,' Rowles answered.

After a telling nod from Jude, Rowles, Fuller and Pipestone wandered away from the small group. Fuller and Rowles said they thought they were owed a drink and went to the Blue Coop with Max and Monte Kinnan. Jude and Pipestone sat on a shaded bench near the small courthouse.

'Well, what's to these rumours, Jude?' Pipestone asked.

'What rumours?'

'I've heard that our sheriff's tried to get you cornered on more'n one occasion. Word is, it's down to the Rickson filly. Is that close?'

'Close enough. But then again, a long way's off. Whatever Bere does next, it ain't because I'm any sort o' rival. An' I ain't expandin' on that.'

Pipestone gave a low, breathy chuckle and sliced himself a fresh chaw. 'Tell me why your Rachel Fletcher was so interested in Bart an' Dooley Susan. She kin to 'em or somethin'?'

Jude shook his head. 'I don't know, Pipe. But she does sound like she's interested in their wellbeing. Perhaps it's just fightin' an' killin' she don't like, an' the Susan family's the nearest we got to it. Except me an' the good sheriff o' course.'

'Hehe,' Pipestone cackled. 'You goin' creek fishin'?'

'I might as well think about it, for all the good work I'm puttin' in around here.'

'Remember to take a gun if you do. I told you once.'

'Yeah I know you did, an' I will. My Colt'll stop anythin' from thirty feet. Not that I aim to get that close, when I'm hookin' steelheads.' After a few moments, Jude gave Pipe a searching look. 'Why don't you light out after the Susans?' he said. 'You're the single best goddamn tracker between here an' the ocean, an' I'll wager you can shoot out most barn doors.'

'The reward'll be temptin', Jude, but bank robbers

71

ain't in my line o' business. What I will do though, is ride down an' see if there's any interestin' sign at Mallit's. From then on, well, who knows.'

As proprietor of the Blue Coop saloon, Corbett Welt carried some political clout in Trinity County. 'You know, it's behoven of my position that I keep an impartial ear to the ground', he was often heard to say, and no doubt one of the reasons the county legislature regularly consulted him on such matters as the election and re-election of district officials. But ironically it was that 'position' that had cost Welt the office of town sheriff. It was rumoured that Ingram Bere had garnered the most votes because Welt had got a few friends in the lowest of places as well as in the higher ones.

Nevertheless, Welt was doing well. He was making money from the Blue Coop, and he was smart enough to know how to keep the best part of it. Only on pay days, high days and holidays was it necessary for himself and other bar staff to stay back all the time. Consequently, at quieter times, he'd walk over to the batwings, flick out crumbs for the mourning doves, and survey the town's movement. That's how he noticed a group of key citizens – stockholders mostly – across the street outside the closed bank. Then he'd seen Jude and Pipestone get up from the bench where they'd sat and talked under the manzanita. 'A few minutes, Jude,' he'd called out and raised a beckoning hand.

Jude thought there might be some useful or cheering news he could take back to his pa. But he knew the stockholders were an unlikely source and he went to see Welt, instead.

'Come in and have a drink on me,' the saloon keeper offered, and held one of the doors open. 'You can't sit an' jabber in the sun *all* day. Mountain goats can, but *you* can't.'

Jude nodded at Rowles and Fuller who were playing blackjack with the Kinnan brothers. Then he took a few tasty swallows of the cool beer that Welt pushed in front of him.

'Is that why you invited me over?' he said. 'To show me how well you can keep beer?'

'Thanks, but not quite,' Welt replied, with a smile of genuine pleasure. 'There's somethin' I want to talk to you about.'

'Yeah? What's that, Corbett?'

'I've been talkin' to Patch Bosun. He's a county administrator. You know him?'

Jude nodded. 'Not well, though. Marketin' ain't what I do most of.'

'Well, he seems to think that Spooner's Drift's without a sheriff. An' he ain't too certain about Saul Pruitt, either.'

'I wonder how he feels about Bill?' Jude muttered, slightly bothered at no mention of Bosun's own son. 'Still, we have got Cappy Rowles. I don't think Peg Fuller's too smitten with law work.'

Welt leaned across the bar counter, took a fleeting

look at the card players. 'Ain't exactly the cut o' the crop, are they?' he suggested. 'Even if Bere does return, he ain't goin' to be viable. Not after all this.' Welt lifted Jude's glass and wiped the bar with his wet cloth. 'But Rowles an' Fuller ain't the only runners,' he hinted.

'Yeah, I know. There's Bill, if he comes back,' Jude responded. 'An' I'd say his votes are guaranteed, if he wants to stand. Is that what you're suggestin', Corbett?'

'Not really. I could give you the name o' ten fellers who'd make a better fist of bein' sheriff than Ingram Bere. An' they'd come with more backbone. But you're right, Jude, that ain't what I've got in mind.'

'Ha, you mean what you an' our county leaders have already discussed,' Jude suddenly realized. 'If it ain't Bosun the younger, are you sayin' it's me?'

'It didn't *quite* happen like that, Jude. They asked me for my opinion. For what it's worth I gave it, an' meant it.'

'Jeesus, Corbett. I've got the reputation of a ne'er-do-well candy-ass, *not* a goddamn town sheriff. I've been upholdin' everythin' *except* the law. For Chris'sakes I've even taken a swing at the face of it. No, you best think again.'

But Jude Linsey had already done some of his own thinking. Just before the bank had been robbed, his father had told him he was on the wastrel's road, and it had sunk in. For the past few years he'd got himself a well-earned reputation for being irresponsible, uninterested in anything that didn't involve his own entertainment. Perhaps it was more about folk turning a blind eye to his peccadilloes, than being liked. From what his pa had said, his ma wasn't too enamoured of him either. So maybe what he'd told Pipestone was wrong. Maybe it was time for him to think about putting something into the town, helping out those people who'd indulged him.

A few thought provoking moments later, Welt's face twisted with a shrewd grin. 'Nope, still can't think of an alternative,' he said. 'An' I ain't acceptin' a categorical refusal either. I just saw your face, an' it spoke to me of a significant interest.'

Jude returned an enigmatic smile. '*Interest* yeah, maybe there is,' he conceded. 'But *significant* might take a bit longer.'

12

From beneath the saloon's broad awning, Jude looked across at the men who were still talking with Ogden Sayler outside of his bank. Now, he'd decided, he really did want to talk with his father. He'd bring him the welcome and cheering news of Patch Bosun's offer. No doubt he'd be better pleased, have something more positive to chew on, regarding Jude's future.

An hour later, Jude was driving the surrey around the black oaks, when he saw two riders out on the west fork of the approach road.

He reined in until the lead rider intercepted him. It was Hank Bosun; the other rider was Saul Pruitt, the deputy sheriff of Spooner's Drift, and he was dead.

'I couldn't do anythin' for him,' Bosun said. 'He took a belly shot an' his horse dragged him a spell. It was as much as I could do to get him back into his saddle. I couldn't leave him out there.'

Jude ground his jaw with anger. 'I thought we

might be seein' you,' he said. He was trying to hide his frustration, could sense the fates closing around him. 'This is first port o' call down from the mountain; like it was for Fuller an' Rowles.'

'You seen 'em? They're back?'

'Yeah, they're back. Ain't left the Blue Coop since. It was the same Susan boys that shot at you?'

'Yeah, who else? We never got to see 'em though. Where's Bere?'

'Why you askin'?' Jude asked, fully aware of the answer.

'He must've known who an' what was waitin' for us up there. He's the goddamn sheriff, so I'd like to ask him about it.'

'Yeah, I just bet you would. I take it you didn't see much of him after the shootin'?'

'No. Curious thing is, not much o' the gunfire went *his* way. An' he was leadin' us . . . along with Saul Pruitt, here. Don't *that* seem kind o' curious?'

'Almost divine, Bill,' Jude agreed. 'So you saw no sign o' the Susans . . . no one?'

Bosun shook his head. 'Neither hide nor hair. An' *you* ain't seen Bere?'

'No. Teller says he saw him for while. Looks like he's done one o' them show acts.'

'Huh. He's gone straight back up the mountain, or I'll eat my own saddle.'

'Thinkin' the worst of him's amusin', an' probably accurate, Bill. Unfortunately it ain't hard evidence in the eyes o' the law.'

'Has anybody gone out after him?' Bosun asked.

'I don't think so.' Jude didn't want to say that Pipestone had gone to look for trail sign. 'We're settin' up a swing station here,' he said. 'You want to come in for some food an' drink?'

'No, I don't think so, Jude. I've got to get word to my folks. Besides, it's heatin' up, an' poor ol' Saul ain't gettin' any fresher.'

After the man had ridden on, Jude walked slowly towards the house. His mother stepped from the scullery door to meet him.

'This is where I normally get offered hot coffee an' biscuits,' he said, trying to maintain a sort of cheer. 'Where's Rachel?' he asked, glancing into the house. 'Do you know if there's anythin' wrong, Ma? Lately, she's actin' mighty odd, like there's a burr under her saddle.'

Elspeth Linsey eyed her son keenly. 'Well, I don't know whether it's any of our business, Jude, but there is somethin' curious, and as you've mentioned it. . . .'

'What sort o' curious, Ma?'

'Well, I couldn't help noticing in her room last week . . . her blanket box with its lid open. There were some things . . . some things that weren't what I'd expect of a working girl . . . our maid.'

'Things, Ma?'

'Fancy-worked dresses, a tray with trinkets, sparkly chokers and the like.'

'Hmm. Looks like we got ourselves a girl with hidden depths,' Jude suggested wryly.

'An' if you look closely at her hands, you'll see they've not been overlong in any wash sink, either. It's the sort of thing a woman notices, Jude. It's something *hidden* all right, and got me to wondering just *what* it was she did before she came here.'

'Well, you could always ask her. Maybe she's that Jersey Lily, down on her luck.'

'All I'm saying is, it's mighty queer. Especially with the way she's been acting lately.'

'You goin' to let her draw pay, Ma?'

'I should. I know that finances aren't too sound right now, but your pa says we can retain her for the time being. Besides that, Jude, I have grown fond of the girl.'

'Yeah, I think we all have. So keep her.' Jude gave his mother's shoulder a gentle squeeze. 'I was goin' to take that roan o' mine for another session o' saddle teach,' he said, 'but maybe I'll give him a little water an' hay instead. I've remembered I got to see a man in town about somethin'.'

In the middle of the afternoon, and under the manzanitas, Jude found Pipestone. He was dozing, stretched out, full-length on one of the plaza benches.

'You been out at the Mallit place? When did you get back?' he asked, tapping the seat with the toe of his boot.

'A while ago,' Pipestone snorted, 'Had me a couple o' drinks. Given a chance, I come here to sleep it off.'

'Well, you done that. Did you find any sign o' Bere?' Jude asked.

'I didn't have much trouble pickin' up his track. It led straight out to Eel Creek. Sign led for about a mile, this side o' the water, then it turned sharp east. Looked like he was set on hittin' the county line somewhere's near Musselback. I followed it for a bit, but then it went into the shallows ... cut straight back up on the other side. It looked like he'd changed his mind an' headed for the Ricksons. Either that, or it's what he meant all the while. But what d'you suppose the varmint did then?'

'I don't feel like supposin', Pipe.'

'He took to the water again. Goddamnit, I could-n't find where him an' his horse come out. There's the shallows up there, but there's a big coil of eels just waitin' in the holes. Some of 'em are as big as your arm.'

'So you never pinned down his trail?'

'No, I didn't. An' ridin up to the Ricksons – if that's where he went – ain't my business.' The old man swung his legs to the ground, rubbed knuckles around his leathery face. 'Now are you goin' to expand on whether you got feelin's for that gal?' he asked.

Jude smiled. 'Yeah, I got feelin's for her, Pipe. I always will have. Trouble is, lately they ain't the right kind. If she sees more in Ingram Bere than *me*, how come? I thought love was blind.'

'Ha, you got me there, son. Perhaps it was somethin' she *heard*,' Pipestone replied, with his rumbling chuckle. 'I don't know spit about that sweetheart stuff. It must be twenty years since I spoke to a woman, let alone had feelin's for one.'

'Someone told me it weren't so long ago, you were mixin' it with a girl from the cat wagon.'

'That's true, but I never actually got to say anythin'. Thinkin' back, perhaps I should've done.' For a few moments, the discomfited mountain man rummaged in his pockets for a chaw. 'Anyways, the *real interestin'* news is,' he continued, 'a little way before I got to where Bere forded the creek, I ran across the fresh tracks of a pair o' grizzlies. I reckon they'd been pawin' fish from the shallows.'

'What? You reckon they ate the sheriff as well?'

'No. They're more goddamn choosy than that. I'm sayin' the trout must be runnin'. What d'you say me an' you head up there? After that, we can go on up to my cabin. I got a mule an' a hound staked out either end of a lungin' rope. I'm hopin' they ain't got 'emselves in a tangle or worse by the time I get back.'

'That's a mighty invitin' offer, Pipe. But I reckon I'll be stayin' here in town. I done some thinkin' an' got a tad more to do. I just reached a fork in my road, or somethin' akin to it.'

Pipestone gave him a deep, perceptive look. Then he waved his hand, turned and strode away without another word.

Jude's thinking included Alice Rickson and Rachel

Fletcher. Besides that, he thought he *would* take a look along Eel Creek. With a bit of luck, he might pick up the trail of the missing sheriff. 'Damn his hide,' he said, almost shouted.

13

It was well into full dark before Forbes Rickson started to unhitch the rig. He was outraged, his mind aggressive. He cared little for what others had lost from the bank, only for what the Susan Boys gang had taken of his. He grunted uncivilly at one of the ranch workers who came to take care of the team, then he walked stiffly from the barn to the house. As he neared the porch, his wife appeared in the light as the door opened.

'Hello, Forbes,' she called out with her everlasting good humour. 'I thought it must be you. Is Alice not with you?'

'No. I thought she'd be here.'

'Well, she's not. Do you think she decided to spend another night with Milly?'

Rickson shook his head irritably. He had seen his daughter in town talking with Milly Pease, late yesterday afternoon. But, other than when he'd had his out of town squabble just before the robbery, he couldn't be sure. 'Yeah, I guess that's it,' he mumbled, 'she's obviously spendin' another night with her. You got any supper for me?'

'Well, put like that, I don't know whether you're sayin' or askin', Forbes. But you come in an' get yourself washed up, an I'll find somethin' to put on the table.'

Not until he was full of pie and potatoes and a high-topped glass of brandy, did Rickson bring himself to tell his wife just how much they'd lost from the robbery.

'Oh, Forbes, that's not a joke, is it?'

'You know jokin' don't come out o' my drawer, May. We've lost just about everythin', an' old Sayler's likely to hold me to the mortgage. Well, he's got another think comin' when he does. He was responsible for the safety o' my money, an' my money is my means to pay.'

'Do you really think he'll do that, Forbes? Take the house from us?'

'He's done it before. Loyalty, or amity, or even bein' a stockholder, don't come into it. He's a banker not a charity. Most of his gains are ill-gotten somewhere down the line. An' in terms o' morality, he's as bad as any gang o' bank robbers.'

Briefly, May Rickson's mind wandered. Life at the ranch was mostly humdrum and routine, and she felt a wrench of envy that Alice should be in town, talking about and soaking up the drama of the robbery.

'Was anybody hurt in the robbery? You never said,'

she asked of her husband.

'Not durin' it. Saul Pruitt got shot when they went after 'em. There's goin' to be a few wasted votes if Ingram Bere ever stands for sheriff again. Our futures were restin' on that posse gettin' my money back.'

'I hope you don't mean that, Forbes. It was a dreadful price to pay. Saul Pruitt's family won't be seein' *their* future like that. At least we've got one.'

'I *do* see it like that, May. It's my money, an' I've been thinkin' about it. Ogden Sayler will see my assets as the bank's assets. That's how it works. They'll see it as *their* loss, not *mine or ours.*'

With silent concern, May smiled tolerantly. Notwithstanding robberies, she wished her husband would occasionally return home in a more gentle, equable humour. It was some sort of man who'd be more worried about his finances than the wellbeing of his own daughter.

Pipestone didn't set out for his cabin as he'd planned. His animals were well accustomed to being left alone. The bank robbery had generated an infamiliar excitement in the town, and he was loath to leave the carry-on and speculation. Up in his cabin, he only had himself to talk to, but in Spooner he could find plenty of willing collaborators for the building of doubtful storylines. Late evening, he went to the livery to see Franklin Teller. He wanted to make sure that his mule was getting its fair share of the oats he would be paying for.

'Put that fork down, Frank,' he advised, after he'd taken a look at the mule. 'You ain't on today's jointin' list. I *was* goin' to suggest a game o' cards, but by Judge Johnson's braces, the smell you're puttin' out would turn a polecat. An' what the hell are you scratchin at?'

'It's the hay chaff. This goddamn stuff's plum full o' foxtail.'

Pipestone shook his head with lack of concern. 'You want to play some cooncan?' he asked. 'I'll nip to the Blue Coop, get us a couple o' packs from Welt, an' a bottle o' tonsil paint.'

'Yeah, why not. But make it one pack an' two bottles. An' bring some o' them canned sardines he keeps. I got some crackers here somewhere.'

Jude didn't disturb Rachel to cook him breakfast. It was before daybreak and he didn't want to involve himself in any uneasy conversation. He wrapped some cheese and corn dodgers in a napkin and grabbed his Colt, a water canteen and his fishing creel. The stars were still shining and, deciding not to use the reata, he only had a little trouble in catching and saddling the roan. 'What you don't see, can't spook you, feller,' he said softly. 'An' I don't care how you smash the stuffin' out of anyone else, just remember I'm the one who gives you board an' lodgin'.'

Jude was clear of the town and beyond the Mallit

spread before light broke across Shell Mountain. Instead of crossing at the ford beyond which were a few of the smaller ranches on the easterly side of the creek, he cut along the west side. From there, he soon picked up the trail left by Pipestone's mule and the horse of the man who'd been followed.

The trail cut northward, as Pipestone had said, then on towards the Rickson ranch which was another five miles. Jude saw other horse tracks of both shod and unshod horses, but he didn't see any sign of the bears that Pipestone had spoken of.

'What the hell was the ol' fool talkin' about?' he grumbled. 'I wish I knew which half of his tales to believe.'

Jude turned the head of the roan towards the foothills. He didn't intend to do any fishing until the following day. He'd make night camp somewhere along the creek narrows, and early tomorrow he'd take the roan on up to the headwater.

14

Six months before the Spooner's Drift bank robbery, Will Lasseter had bought a section of grazing land in an ox bow of Eel Creek about twenty miles north-west of the town. He'd built a cabin and barns from green pine; along with about a hundred head of cattle, established himself, his wife and two children. Reaching the town by wagon road was an tortuous, rough journey of ten miles to connect with the south-north road. Consequently, when Lasseter needed supplies, he took a horse and sawbucked mule along an old pack trail that led down from the upper end of the Bull Chop.

About the same time that Jude Linsey was setting off to fish the creek, Lasseter was breaking trail, weaving through a thicket of scrub oak. With its bridle reins tangled in low brush, the buckskin mare he'd seen, was standing unresponsive and dejected, about fifty yards ahead.

'Hell of a hitchin' stand,' he said, on riding closer.

He edged his cow pony in, and grimacing, leaned over and eased up one of the buckskin's stirrups. The flesh around the cinch was swollen to such an degree that the edges of the belly strap were hardly visible. 'You want to inflict sufferin', this is the way to do it,' he muttered crossly.

The saddle was of a size that suggested to Lasseter that the rider was a youngster, the stirrups set too high for a man of even middling height. 'Must've been here for a while,' he pondered. 'Whoever was ridin' this poor mount, must've been some sort o' pilgrim. Why the hell didn't they at least take a few holes out o' the cinch?'

Lasseter heeled the pony into a broad circle to look for boot tracks, but he didn't see any. Going back to the buckskin, he dismounted to examine its saddle more carefully. These are bloodstains, he told himself, looking at some dry, dark patches on the polished leather. 'An' if only you could talk,' he said.

He was about to unsaddle the buckskin when, feeling uneasy about the situation, he changed his mind. He loosened the cinch a couple of notches, then moved and retied the reins to where the horse could chomp a tuft of wheat-grass. Next, he led the pony and the pack mule along the trail the buckskin was making, before getting snarled in the brush.

Less than a hundred yards on, Lasseter stopped. Just off and below the trail, he saw an out-of-place bundle of muted colour. 'I think we're here,' he said. He made a knot of his animals' bridle reins, and, leaving them hitched together, he drew out his old Army Colt and made his way quickly down the rough, grassy slope. He could see now it was the body of a woman, and he cursed. 'Yeah, a woman . . . should've realized,' he said. Then he saw that it wasn't being thrown from the buckskin that had killed her. A bullet had taken out her left eye; a mortal wound that was now a pool of black, congealed blood.

Lasseter took a few deep breaths. 'She ain't no more'n a goddamn kid.' He looked around, then back at the girl, noticed her torn, rumpled clothing. 'Don't take a John Pinkerton to work out what's happened here,' he muttered disgustedly. From the look of the ash and embers, he saw that the fire had obviously been kindled more than once. 'Someone must've been here through the night,' he said, feeling awkward and vulnerable. 'What the hell's goin' on? Christ, what the hell's goin' on?'

He kicked at a charred, oak branch, realized the warm ashes could have been that way for many hours. There was a sapling nearby that had had its slim branches stripped. It's where the grey pulled itself away, he thought, seeing the chewed grass around the roots of the young tree.

From then on, it didn't take Lasseter long to find another set of prints. They were bigger, likely from a good-sized, heavily built man. He also saw the hoof marks of a second horse.

Lasseter continued with his futile questions and cursing. He levered a cartridge into the breech of his rifle, stomped around looking at the scuffed and kicked-up ground. 'She must've got shot after a fight, or whatever,' he continued, as if he needed the reason. But there was nothing more, and he turned back to the body and kneeled. The girl's arm was turned awkwardly beneath her and, curious, Lasseter lifted a fold in the rust coloured skirt. The gloved hand was pushed into the soft ground, but between the small fingers, polished metal suddenly glinted in the day's early light.

'Christ, what the hell *did* happen here?' he gasped, got to his feet and took a step back. 'I'm out o' this place, an' I wish I hadn't seen *that*.'

Two hours later, Will Lasseter tied his mounts to the hitch rack in front of the Ranchers' Foodstuffs and General Trading store. Noel Linsey was the first man he'd traded with when he'd first arrived in the Bull Chop valley. The proprietor had assured him that if ever he wanted or needed credit, he could have it.

'Hello, Will,' Linsey said, as soon as the door bell pinged. 'Here for the usual?'

'That's the way it was when I set out,' Lasseter responded fretfully.

'Oh? Somethin' changed your mind?'

'Yeah, on the way in. If you've got a minute, Noel, I've got to tell.'

'I'm not expectin' to get busy for an hour or so yet, Will. What's got you so agitated?'

Linsey was badly shaken badly by Lasseter's story. 'I

can see why you're tellin' me, an' not goin' to the obvious place,' he responded. 'Not as if there is one . . . eh?'

'No. What the hell was I supposed to say? I don't really know what I been lookin' at. Mind's been turnin' it over. I know what it was I saw, but. . . .'

'An' I don't *understand*, Will. It's Alice Rickson you're talkin' about. It's got to be. But I thought she'd gone home after the bank robbery. It would've been *some time* after, but I'm sure that's where she went. Her an' Jude had a fallin' out over somethin'.' Linsey was shaking his head in disbelief 'What the hell was she doin' out there, anyway? It's off the track to or from her home. We got to send someone to let her ma an' pa know. You're sure she was dead, Will?'

'O' course I'm sure. She had half the front of her face shot away,' Lasseter blurted out nervously.

'Yeah, OK Will, I'm sorry. But we ain't got any law officers to speak of. None that can handle this sort o' crime. We can go an' see the doc. He is the circuit coroner. First we'll go to the mercantile, an' see Patch Bosun. He don't carry a pistol, but he's the nearest we got to law at the moment,' Linsey offered.

15

When the two men came from Bosun's Mercantile twenty minutes later, Patch Bosun was with them. As the three men walked purposefully across the street, Linsey considered what Jude would have done in the circumstances, how his son would handle being town sheriff. Maybe just for once, he's best off on his goddamn fishin' trip, he thought drily.

'I guess this shouldn't come as too much of a surprise,' Dr Ralph Wishnak said, after hearing Lasseter's story. 'Well, not those of us who've seen what's goin' on between the two of 'em,' he added, during the immediate, uneasy silence. 'Sorry gentlemen, but doctors' ain't immune.'

'No, that's obvious,' Lasseter, said, taken aback at Wishnak's blunt assumption.

'You wouldn't be so shocked if it was the diagnosis of a drunken hay hand,' the doc stated, and just as forthright.

'Yes, I would.' Linsey contributed. 'An' it's goin' to

come as a bit of a shock to her parents an' my boy.'

'Yeah,' Bosun agreed, looking sympathetically at Linsey. 'This ain't what normally comes about between a couple o' love-lorns, is it? Even if it is bein' kept a secret.'

'It often is when one of 'em stakes a claim on someone else's territory. After the mistakes you make in *your* lives, you get back on your feet, dust yourself off, an' start over. *I'm* more used to callin' out the undertaker.'

'The Rickson girl made a goddamn mistake all right,' Linsey snorted angrily. 'An' Ingram Bere's goin' to, when we find him.'

'If there's someone capable o' that sort o' killin', I'm gettin' straight back to my family,' Lasseter decided.

'Yeah, o' course,' Wishnak agreed. 'But don't get too anxious. If you commit that sort o' crime, you're probably goin' to avoid most folk.'

'Yeah? Well, *most* ain't certain enough for me,' Lasseter replied. 'I'd like to shoot him on sight.'

'If it *was* him, you'll get to see him hanged,' Bosun said. 'Meantime, we got to run him down, an' I'm suggestin' we enlist the help of Pipestone.'

'Christ, Patch, that ol' duffer's likely to kick the bucket before he reaches the timberline. Besides, he ain't in town.'

'He is,' corrected the doctor. 'I saw him not half an hour ago, catchin' forty winks outside the court-house. Either that, or he's turned to stone an' no one's noticed.'

'Let's go see,' Patch Bosun put in.

'Shouldn't we send someone out to tell the Ricksons?' Linsey asked. 'Someone has to. They'll want to bring the girl in ... take her back to the ranch, maybe ... I don't know.'

'Don't worry, I'll take care o' that,' Wishnak said.

Lying on the plaza bench, Pipestone was playing possum. He was still trying to make sense of the section of Bere's trail that he'd followed, couldn't understand what the sheriff had taken to the creek water for. Then, from the corner of a crinkled eyelid, he saw Linsey, Bosun and Lasseter approach him.

'I know two o' you,' he said, hardly moving.

'This is Will Lasseter,' Bosun said, in response, 'an' we need your help.'

When Lasseter stretched out a hand, Pipestone took it and pulled himself to a sitting position. 'Howdy,' he gruffed out, and gave a snaggle-toothed grin.

'Somethin' bad's happened, Pipe, somethin' that needs your particular expertise,' Bosun started to explain.

'Huh, that ain't too specific. I can shoot someone for you, or cut 'em up for dog meat, but long, hard work ain't my line o' business any more.'

'The person involved's already been shot. We want you to track their killer,' Bosun informed him. 'Lasseter here will fill you in.'

As Lasseter related his story again, Pipestone made

sense out of every crooked and devious trail that Sheriff Ingram Bere had laid on his ride from town. Pipestone too, considered Jude Linsey's help, but this was a delicate circumstance, and he thought there was more to be gained from Jude tracking those grizzly bears.

'An' you're sure you saw what you're sayin' you saw?' he asked of Lasseter.

'Yeah, I'm sure. The badge was torn from a sheriff's vest. Considerin' what he was doin', he probably didn't notice. Otherwise he'd've come back for it.'

'One day soon he's goin' to wish he did. Was the girl assaulted?' Pipestone asked.

'Yeah, it looked like maybe she was. It weren't no language o' love that I know of.'

'I'll need a couple o' men to ride up there with,' Pipestone decided abruptly. 'I ain't quite the mountain goat I used to be.'

Just look like it, was Bosun and Linsey's shared thought. 'Who do you want?' Linsey asked.

Pipestone looked to Bosun. 'Well that boy o' yours, Hank,' he said. 'Cappy Rowles too. Get him out o' the Blue Coop, an' he's almost as good as new. They're both sworn in for some lawful backin'.'

'You'll want spare horses with food an' beddin'?'

'No. If them two are comin' they'll need nothin' extra. This'll be a ride to manage without. Do you want me to shoot Bere?'

'Oh yes,' Noel Linsey said.

'Only if you have to,' Bosun said, with a cheerless

shake of his head. 'But I'll back your judgement.'

'One more thing,' Pipestone said. 'I'll want full sheriff's pay for as long as it takes.'

'You'll get it,' Linsey confirmed bluntly.

16

Using a fresh cut switch for a rod, Jude was crouching low, keeping his shadow away from the slow swirling creekside pool. He flicked out a cutworm, watched it splash on to the surface of the water, then he smiled. But it wasn't for a fish he'd caught, simply the dawning of Pipestone's explanation for the two sets of fresh bear tracks. In a momentary flash, Jude realized there weren't any grizzly bears, and never had been. It was the prints of four riders that Pipestone was obliquely referring to; the men who were now closing in on him as he cast a line for a young steelhead.

He cursed silently when he heard the troubled snort of the roan. Then he sighed and lifted the rod. 'I'm just drawin' in the bait,' he called out. 'So whoever's back there, don't get to thinkin' otherwise.'

'I hear you. You just carry on,' a voice came back

from close behind him.

Jude cursed again. After having ambushed the sheriff's posse, the Susan Boys gang had headed north, then crossed the Bull Chop to the westerly range in order to get where they were now.

Many thoughts turned around in Jude's head as he fitted another worm to the hook, forced calm on himself to recast. But before the bait had time to sink, a fat trout took it, and the man behind him laughed.

'That's a real nice-lookin' fish. Land another one, an' we'll all have a tasty spread. Go on, boy, catch 'im,' the man rasped.

Jude flicked another cutworm out to the far edge of the pool. But he'd hardly waited a few seconds before another fish broke the surface, having taken the bait in its wolf-like jaws. Jude was hauling the meaty, fighting fish from the water, when he felt his Colt being drawn from his holster.

'You got anythin' else?' the voice asked.

'Only my knife.'

'Keep it. You'll need it to gut these fish, nothin' else.'

Jude turned around slowly to confront a tall, darkly featured man who standing directly behind him. The man was dressed plain, had long hair and a heavy moustache. Jude stared for longer than he would normally have done, because he was instantly reminded of someone.

'What were you expectin'?' the man said, 'some

sort o' raggedy-assed trail bum? I'm Dooley Susan.'

'Yeah, I'd already guessed most of it,' Jude agreed. 'Where's the rest o' your gang?'

'Right here,' Dooley said, and held out his hand to indicate three other men who were advancing from cover of the willow grove. 'The lucky one who looks like me's Bart. He's my brother.'

All the men were soberly dressed, and looked calm. One of them wore a brace of Colts, another carried a Winchester carbine. Jude took in their self-assurance; not one of them had drawn or levelled a gun.

The man with the carbine had a long black scarf tied loosely around his neck. 'We snuck up on you easy enough, feller,' he said, nodding almost sociable like. 'Are you ill-informed, or merely mindin' your own business?'

'Not really,' Jude answered him. 'A man's got to eat.'

'I'd say he's a lawman,' the other one said, blinking menacing, pale-grey eyes.

'An' I'm guessin' you're the one they call Ghost Mower,' Jude retorted. 'So are you goin' to shoot me now, or wait till I've cooked what I've caught?' he added.

'Hah. What's your name?' Bart asked.

'Linsey. Jude Linsey, an' I've come up here to fish.'

'Well, Jude Linsey, we ain't killers. Sure we killed, but only when interferin' folk gave us no quarter. My pa always said never to interfere with nothin' that don't bother you.'

'Yeah, I know what he meant,' Jude replied meaningfully. 'Only the other day, I was sayin' a similar thing to the townsfolk o' Spooner's Drift.'

For a moment, Bart Susan contemplated Jude's remark. 'It's a way o' stayin' alive,' he suggested with a thin, wily smile.

After they'd eaten the steelheads and taken coffee, the bank robbers openly discussed what was to be done with Jude.

'We can keep him till tomorrow . . . make up our minds *then*,' the man who was called Dese Dawter recommended. 'Bart already told him we ain't killers.'

'Yeah, OK. Let's all hope I don't live to regret it,' Bart said, and took a hard, calculating look at Jude.

'You mean you hope you don't *die* regrettin' it,' Dooley advised. 'He stays until the mornin'.'

As the men talked on into the night, they took it in turns to keep the fire refuelled. Jude hoped that Pipestone would emerge from the darkness, knew that when the gang members did sleep, they wouldn't all do it at the same time. He was aware that they were wanted men, dead or alive. The price on their head was enough to stop them mistaking confidence for carelessness.

'Hey, Linsey,' Dooley Susan said, 'what do you do for a livin' when you ain't takin' a vacation?'

'As little as I can get away with,' Jude answered. 'I

have been known to do some horse an' cow work. Mostly I live off an allowance. It's enough for the essentials.'

'I don't believe I've ever had the pleasure of such a life,' Bart said, but without sounding impressed.

Jude didn't think now was the time or place to talk about his reaching a crossroads, that his mind was made up about becoming the Spooner's Drift sheriff elect. 'Gettin' rich at a dollar a day takes a long time. Then you'd all know that,' Jude replied, with a tired, exasperated laugh.

'Yeah, a hell of a long time,' Dooley agreed. 'Nobody but a fool would try it that way. We're all for the stickin' up of a train or bank alternative. We'd rather get shot, than have to work for twelve hours every goddamn day.'

It was clear to Jude that whilst Dooley was the gang's boss and decision maker, Dese Dawter and Ghost Mower weren't along solely to take orders. They were obviously proficient at their chosen trade, and in their own lawbreaking ways, probably loyal.

What Jude needed was some sort of distraction, a clash within the camp. But they were too smart to fall for anything badly devised, he was thinking. He knew he wasn't walking away scot free, more a question of how long he'd got to live. And the longer he stayed, the more reason there'd be to shut him up.

'We'll bring the blankets over,' Dooley said. 'This

looks as good a place as any to camp. Near the pools too, for one of Mr Linsey's breakfasts.'

'I'm gettin' tired o' camp cookin',' Dese Dawter responded. 'I'd like some fine city fixin's. Does anyone remember them times?'

'Yeah. The Cherry Dame in Sacramento,' Dooley recalled with a sigh. 'A plum in one hand, an' a—'

'Careful, Dooley,' Bart interrupted. 'That sort o' dreamin' can turn to risk takin'. Unless we take real care, we'll never eat again *anywhere*, let alone Sacramento,' he warned his brother.

It was only when Mower and Dawter returned with blankets and other gear ten minutes later, that Jude realized he'd made his fishing camp less than a hundred yards from where the Susans had already pitched theirs.

Bart took a length of rope from Dawter and contemplated Jude's predicament. 'Do you mind bein' tied up hand and foot for the night?' he asked.

Jude shrugged, smiled crookedly. 'No, an' it's right neighbourly o' you to ask. I hear there's a street in Sacramento where you pay for that sort o' stuff. Besides, what *I* say ain't goin' to make much difference.'

'No difference,' Bart confirmed tersely. 'I won't tie your hands *behind* your back, 'cause Ghost's goin' to be watchin' you till midnight. That's right, ain't it, Ghost?' he said.

'Yeah,' Ghost confirmed. 'I'll call Dooley, an' at about three, he can call you. Dese takes first duty

103

tomorrow, if the fisherman's still our guest,' he snarled.

'He will be,' Dooley said, without giving anything away. 'I'll think about all our fates in the mornin'.'

17

A little before dawn, Jude was stiff and sore from his cramped position. He rolled on to his side, saw the small camp-fire that had been his own had burned down to ash. Bart Susan sat hunched and unmoving not far away, and Jude guessed that he and his brother had changed their night guard shift.

'Hey,' Jude called, forcing out an evenly tempered sound. 'How about takin' these ropes off me? I'd like to get some circulation goin'.'

'Yea, OK,' Bart mumbled, coming out of his doze. 'You've had most o' the night, I'd've thought a resourceful young dude like you woulda done it himself.'

'No, I didn't want to tempt you. Besides, I was too busy dreamin' you choked on a fishbone,' Jude said.

'Ha. You keep up your good humour, Linsey. You'll need it when Ghost wakes up.'

'Don't go turnin' him loose just yet, Bart,' Dooley called out. 'Wait till we get our boots on.'

Jude realized then that he'd made the mistake of not taking his off. His hands and feet had swollen. Dawter and Ghost took a sullen stomp around the camp, but seemed to feel better after they'd taken long pulls from their flasks.

Bart threw an armful of brush on to the dying embers and, within moments, the fire was crackling, sending up licks of bright yellow flame. Jude sat down and wrenched off his boots, walked around for a few minutes in his stockinged feet.

Dooley asked Dawter and Ghost to go fetch their supplies. 'An' bring back our coffee pot. This feller's ain't big enough to slake the thirst of a cricket.'

When the two bank robbers had returned with their various tins of foodstuff, Dooley suggested that Jude prepare flapjacks, bacon and coffee for breakfast.

'This is goin' to keep me alive, is it?' Jude asked.

Dooley nodded. 'For a while. Ghost will shoot you as soon as spit, if you don't.'

While Bart had been untying his wrists, Jude had wondered if there was any gain from being either good- or bad-natured if you were going to die anyway. He came to the conclusion that awkward and resentful was more natural, but being camp cook wasn't half as bad as being shot dead.

An hour later, after they'd sipped hot coffee laced with molasses, Ghost and Dawter brought in the horses. Jude's roan was led in, crow-hopping and snorting.

'What sort o' saddle-broke you got here?' Ghost rasped. 'Brute nearly chewed through my arm.'

'Yeah, he's the meanest son-of-a-bitch I ever turned a saddle on,' Jude replied. 'Up to a couple o' weeks ago, no one had ever ridden him. Reckon I'm the only one who can.'

'Well, ain't that a challenge to our own little rodeo clown?' Dawter chuckled. 'You been heard to brag o' no horse ever pilin' you, Ghost. So why not climb this bronc while the vinegar's still in him?'

'I will when I'm good an' ready,' Ghost accepted. 'Right now, the boss wants us to clear for movin' out. The horse will wait.'

'Yeah that's right,' Dooley said. 'Somethin' for us all to look forward to. Why don't you both go an' check the stash, while me an Bart strike what's left o' this camp. Perhaps Mr Linsey weren't on his own up here pond fishin'.'

Jude shook his head and smiled tolerantly. 'I never came up here with anyone. Don't you reckon you'd know by now if I had've done?'

If Jude had reckoned on riding the roan under cover of the outlaws' guns without being tied, he was soon disappointed. Dooley had a picket rope passed back from the saddle horn of his claybank, to Jude's wrists.

'I'll lead us out,' he said.

Ten minutes later the riders passed within a few yards of the gang's first camp. Bart Susan and Dese Dawter dismounted, and Jude discovered just where they'd been keeping their stolen money.

Just about seals my fate, was his first bleak thought.

With Ghost Mower holding their horses' reins, Dawter and Bart pushed aside the root ball of a fallen oak. They reached down and drew out four small canvas sacks, and Jude knew it was the spoils of the Spooner's Drift bank raid, no doubt some of it his own father's cash money.

From then on, the gang didn't intend leaving a clear trail. Dooley led Jude's horse, and dodging through thickets of timber and brush, he zigzagged them up the middle of the valley. Where the trail widened, Dooley held up for Jude to ride alongside him.

The talk was mostly of Dooley attempting to pardon himself and his brother from being named killers. Jude knew it, but didn't understand the point if they'd got him down for a morning execution. But daybreak had started way back. If it was for Dooley to continue pardoning himself, Jude was presently riding on borrowed time.

'Yessir,' Dooley said. 'There's worse things. If I could see my life over, I wouldn't change much. Go for the Cattlemen's Deposits maybe, instead of all these one-horse, money-box towns.'

Inexplicably, Dooley was calling Jude's attention to the new, bigger profits from a future on the owl-hoot trail. Well, he mused, it might have its advantages, especially if a man didn't shrink from getting himself killed, or spending the rest of his life penned up.

Outlawry might have greater perks than being a very dead prospective sheriff. And, according to his father, some sort of outlaw life was beginning to look like the next inevitable step up from Jude's present one.

Occasionally, Jude met the eyes of another man riding behind. They all wore Colts, and carried rifles across their saddles. As well as the sentinel attentions of Dooley, and the psychotic nature of Ghost Mower, he guessed he was never out of the sight of one or another of them.

They came to the foot of a series of hogback ridges. To the left and right the country was thicket-brushed and timbered. It was an old trappers' trail that weaved along and up and down the ridges. It was the trail he'd intended to travel on his way up to the headwaters; the direction that Pipestone had tried to tell him the four men were headed. Well, he mused wryly, maybe he'd get to where the finger trout played, after all.

The trail was so narrow and overgrown in places, that Jude was forced to close in tight on Dooley. The others moved up as well, and several times, Jude had to calm the anxious roan by low, soothing words. He didn't want the horse to show his prowess as a highly strung, gut twister. It wouldn't be too long before Ghost Mower would want to ride him, and Jude didn't want the man to reconsider.

Jude told himself that his best hope was to go on with his captors to wherever they intended to go.

Once there, he could take his time in deciding how he was to get away. He knew that any foolishness or brash bravery would mean instant death. He'd decided that he didn't want to die. He knew it now, wanted to live to tell his ma and pa of his decision. They'd just love it, even if he had spent some time riding with the killer outlaws, camping out in their Robber's Roost.

18

'It'd be mighty easy for a pack o' fool folk to blame the killin' o' that gal on to somebody else. Specially if someone was to flame their touch papers,' Pipestone warned.

Patch Bosun shook his head forcefully. 'They don't have to be *fool folk*, Pipe,' he said. '*Angry ones* would fit the bill. Lasseter, are you proof positive o' that badge?'

'Yeah. What the hell else could it have been with letters spellin' out "SHERIFF"?' the rancher responded. 'You'll be seein' it for yourself shortly.'

Will Lasseter went back to the trading store with Noel Linsey to collect and load up his goods. Without wasting any time, he loaded them on to the pack mule, threw a couple of tight hitches across the saw-buck. Within fifteen minutes he was followed out of town by Pipestone, Hank Bosun and Cappy Rowles. They were all well mounted, each of them packing a blanket and a small amount of food in their saddle-bags.

A half hour after their departure, Ralph Wishnak left in a springy floored buckboard. He had a saddle-horse hitched to the rear and, on arriving at the trail Lasseter was to take, he met all the other horsemen.

'Can we take the buggy right to where she is?' he asked.

'Yeah, most o' the way, I'm sure,' Lasseter said.

'Good, let's go.'

It was a tight, twisted trail, but after considerable manoeuvring and back-tracking, Wishnak managed to stop the rig within sixty feet of where the girl's body lay.

'That's one o' my covers I put on her. I thought it might keep off the buzzards,' Lasseter explained. 'I was careful not to touch anythin' else. Nothin' more'n where she's holdin' the badge. You goin' to have a look, Mr Pipestone?'

'Yeah. An' don't call me *mister*.'

The other men hung back, let Pipestone take a look under Lasseter's canvas. Then they watched quietly as he went carefully over the ground around the girl's body. For two or three minutes, the old man cursed and muttered to himself as he checked the soil's features for dips and dents.

'Where's the girl's horse?' he asked eventually.

'Near,' Lasseter answered. 'But it ain't goin' anywhere. If we set it loose, it'll follow on . . . find its own way home.'

'As long as it don't arrive before one of us does,'

Pipestone said. 'As for the sign *here*, besides the girl an' Lasseter's, there's only been one other set o' boots that's trod this ground. Whoever that is, he's carryin' a tad more lard. An' I'm *that* good, I can almost tell you how much.'

Because of the absence of Ingram Bere, the doctor was now officiating as sheriff as well as coroner. 'Are you sure it's one man who did the murder?' he asked in those capacities.

'If you're rulin' out a suicide, an' Lasseter here, then yeah, we're lookin' for one man,' Pipestone confirmed. 'An' that's Sheriff Bere.'

'How'd you know that?' Cappy Rowles asked.

Pipestone pointed to a shallow depression in the thin, dusty soil. When both Rowles and Hank Bosun had dismounted to take a look, he explained in detail how it was one of the hoofmarks he'd trailed from Vaughan Mallit's pasture. It led from where its rider had put it into the creek water a few miles north of the town.

'And that was Bere?' Rowles asked.

'Yeah. If you want proof, I'll backtrack.'

'Why would Alice Rickson be meetin' anyone up here?' Bosun asked. 'An' she waited all night. There must have been some arrangement.'

'We'll probably never know,' Wishnak said. 'I'll take her down to the Ricksons on the way back. It's best that I take her.'

'What if Bere returns?' Rowles cautioned. 'You'll need a lawful gun with you.'

113

'I'll be all right, thanks. Besides, he ain't ever comin' back here,' Wishnak replied. 'Can you come into town tomorrow, Lasseter?' he asked of the rancher. 'I want you to do some testifyin' for the inquest.'

'Inquest?' Pipestone snapped. 'Judas priest, the girl's got a bullet in her brain. What the hell do you need one o' them for?'

'I've got to satisfy the law, we all know that. Just look on it as the boot that kicks away the trap door.'

'Yeah, I'll be there, Doc,' Lasseter said, upholding Wishnak's authority.

'Good. How long for you to overhaul Bere?' Wishnak asked Pipestone.

'After this piece o' work, he'll be forkin' it somewhere to the tall timber. An' he's goin' to mess up his sign a lot more than he did before. But we'll catch him, don't fear . . . just really can't say when.'

Lasseter helped Wishnak carry the girl's body to the buckboard. 'I'd like to get my hands on that goddamn sheriff,' he rasped, turning under the edges of the canvas wrap. 'There's somethin' I learned to do to unwanted bull calves come to mind. It's a waste of a trial. You sure set on it, Doc?'

'All I can say is – and this ain't to go any further – I'm not against a lynchin' if there's no doubt. But I'm afraid there is one. Not much, but there is.'

'Yeah, we need Bere to confirm what he did, an' that's why we'll catch him,' Pipestone stated with conviction. 'I just hope he don't put up too much of a fight an' we have to shoot him.'

'If you *do*, just get your stories right,' Wishnak advised sternly.

'Before we start out, I'd like you an' me have a word in private,' Pipestone said. 'Cappy, why don't you an' Hank climb your saddles an' ride along with Lasseter an' the buggy a spell. Me an' the doc'll catch you up.'

After the buckboard and the two horsemen had disappeared from sight, Pipestone and Wishnak sat in the dappled shade of a stunted oak.

'It's about Forbes Rickson,' Pipestone started off 'You know how he gets his hackles standin'? Well, he'll raise dust when you ride in with his daughter. He might have lost some cash at the bank, but he'll have enough stuffed in his mattress to buy a mighty big retribution.'

'I think you're right,' the doc agreed. 'Not that we could blame him. But he's a tetchy ol' bird at the best o' times. What can I do?'

'Get a few men posted where they can stop anythin' he sets up. Go to the Blue Coop, an' ask Welt for help. Rickson will be tellin' any mob he gets together, to shoot first. I wouldn't want to be *anyone* in his way. An' I ain't forgot them Susan Boys, either. They could still be within his compass. You got to snuff out his attack.'

'Are those bank robbers implicated in this?' Wishnak asked.

'Yeah. It was them who Bere was meetin' when he

rode beyond the Eel Creek shallows. That's when he snarled his tracks an' rode up here to see the girl. The Susans went downstream, forded the creek an' headed out towards the timberline.'

'Huh? You've known all along that that's where the gang is? You never told anybody? Why the hell not?' Wishnak railed at Pipestone's disclosure.

' 'Cause the whole town would've set off, up an' into them trees, an' never have even caught a squirrel. It would've all been for nothin', except to drive 'em further from the chances o' catchin' 'em. But I did tell *someone*,' Pipestone admitted. 'It weren't direct, but he's smart enough to have worked it out by now.'

'Who are you talkin' about, Pipe?'

'Jude Linsey.'

'Christ. He's a sort o' game hunter now, is he?'

'Well it's only been beaver an' steelheads before. But to my way o' reckonin', yeah, that's what he's doin'. An' for the time bein', Doc, keep it to yourself. Last thing we want is for these hills to be crawlin' with trigger-happy farmers an' storekeepers.'

'I won't tell anyone, Pipe,' Wishnak agreed. 'So Jude Linsey's gone after the Susans? How'd you know where they're headed? What did you tell him?'

'A couple o' weeks ago, I stumbled on a new built cabin. It was a good size, made o' green timber, an' hidden away up near the headwaters. I'd never heard or seen anybody up there. It was only after the robbery I thought about it. That, an' the sign I'd seen. I put two an' two together, realized that's where they'll be goin'. They've probably got a string of 'em all along the coast ranges.'

Wishnak looked suitably taken aback. 'An' you sent young Linsey up there on his lonesome to fetch 'em out?' he asked in amazement.

'Yeah, that or join 'em. He's a capable youngster, an' he didn't have to go.'

'For some reason he did, an' you probably knew it, Pipe. So I'm sorry I can't agree with you. He's runnin' with the wolves.'

'Ah hell, Doc, if he don't turn up soon, I'll go an' bring him in.'

'Like we're doin' with the Rickson girl?' Wishnak retorted coolly.

19

It was nearly mid morning when Jude and his captors crested the last ridge in the string of hog-backs. The five sat their saddles, looked out across a land of fir-clad hills and gullies, where mountain-locked valleys broke into the lush grassland at the northern end of the Bull Chop.

'Why not let me do my own ridin'?' Jude suggested to Dooley Susan. 'I'm too goddamn tired an' achin' to ride off anywhere, if that's what you're worried about.'

'Not just yet, friend,' Dooley replied. 'Right now, what you got to say ain't worth a plugged nickel. I ain't brought you this far to watch you even *tryin'* to ride off.'

'Hey Dooley, it's bringin' him *this* far that's goin' to bring us trouble,' Ghost Mower complained. 'He ain't no use, an' there's probably riders out lookin' for him.'

'Shut up, Ghost,' Dooley turned in the saddle and

shouted back. 'I know all that, but if my plans shape up, he will be o' use. At the moment he only gets shot if an' when he brings it on himself. An' remember I'm still makin' decisions.'

Ahead of them was the drop from the last of the ridges. Confidently, Dooley led the way down the narrow trail and Jude had to follow.

It was a chance to get away, Jude mused, if only Dooley would break from the others. He'd set the roan on its haunches and jerk Dooley's horse from its feet. He'd roll from his saddle and get to Dooley before he could recover himself. But it was only worth the risk if there weren't three armed men behind him. He didn't know for how long, but for the time being, he'd have to wait and watch.

They walked into a densely brushed trail along the easterly side of a gulch that Jude knew was a tributary off Eel Creek. This and the hog-backs were part of old forging trails that stretched between the Bull Chop and Rio Dell Scotia. After half an hour of crooked going they came closer to where the creek widened in its draining of the valley. The water wasn't yet deep, but it ran swift. They turned along the turbulent run, kept to the shale on the west side, where their tracks would be kept to a minimum. To Jude, it was obviously a trail that led to and from wherever they were all headed.

Another mile on, and they were finally reaching the upper end of the creek. Now, and on either side of the bright watercourse, fertile meadows rolled far to the west. It was up here, and on Pipestone's say-so, that Jude would have made his own fishing camp.

'Go on, let me fish for a bit, why don't you?' Jude suggested once again. 'There's trout runnin' here . . . eels, maybe a fat catfish.'

Dooley laughed. 'Hah, even a bank-robbin' city boy knows there ain't any catfish up here, Linsey. But you just keep tryin'.'

'Hey Dooley, a few fine rainbows would go down nicely. It's almost noon,' Ghost called out.

'There won't be any noonin' time today,' Dooley rasped back. 'We're pushin' on.'

Ghost and Dese Dawter muttered at Dooley's decision, but Jude couldn't hear what they said. He doubted protest or complaining was an ongoing attitude, or that it would lead to anything more serious. They were all of them physically and mentally drained at the end of a long campaign. Jude guessed that no amount of squirrelled away gold kept you going for ever.

They picked their way through a brushy, rock-strewn gully. The horses clattered and slipped over the shale, then pushed their way through dry manzanita. What a place for an obliging, chasing fire, Jude told himself. Pressed by a north wind, there'd be no stopping it until it broke through the border brakes.

Late in the afternoon Dooley called for a halt. They dismounted in a glade where the air was heavy, pungently spiced with the smell of pepperwood. But no matter whether they travelled or rested, Jude wasn't once afforded the opportunity of escape.

'God, I'm hungry,' Dese took it as his turn to find something to complain about.

'Hell, we all been thinkin' the same thing, Dese,' Bart supported.

'Not quite the same thing,' Ghost corrected. 'The drawback in this outfit's that we ain't too long on skirt-chasin',' he groused.

'Well it's the *one* thing we agreed on,' Dooley said. 'As long as we hit the outlaw trail, there'd be none o' that. After we've made our pile and split up, every man can do as he pleases. For the moment, save yourself a good-lookin' trout to kiss.'

'I never intended to go without them comforts so long,' Bart joined in. 'I ain't endin' up playin' buck nun. Pretty soon, I'm gettin' me a little crib girl up in Whiskeytown.'

'One?' Dese Dawter put in. 'I'm sendin' off for half-a-dozen o' them catalogue women.'

'Get to your saddles, men,' Dooley said. 'Put the bridle on your roan, Linsey. This was our last stop. You don't have to be led by me any more.'

Jude didn't appreciate having to suddenly guide his own horse. But the roan was nervously tired, and for a time, yielded to downright saddle broke. The men rode in silence, and once again, Jude got to thinking about his predicament and fate. The way he saw it, the gang had already close-shaved with law from Spooner's Drift. And because of the outcome, there'd soon be another chasing group on their heels. So that must be it, Dooley Susan's reasoning. The man wanted him as their rearguard hostage, probably a goddamn shield against a posse's bullets.

When first dark descended on the long valley, the riders were emerging from a stand of tall cypress firs. The sun dropped behind Shell Mountain and settled the land into colourless shadows.

'We're just about there,' Dooley said, but it was with little emotion. The men were so tired now, there was little response.

20

Bart Susan leaned from his horse and dragged open a latch gate that was barely visible to any other approaching rider. All the men rode through, and ahead of them, Jude could just discern a broad meadow maybe a quarter-mile in length and 200 yards wide. The grass was fed by abundant spring water, and was long and green and rich. The entire glade was fringed with pine, ash and more cypress stands. The spread was well concealed from potential observers, anyone riding line from the large ranches at that far northern end of the valley.

Under the failing light, Jude didn't see the cabin at first. Then he saw the low, blocky structure of unpeeled juniper logs that was skilfully protected by a cypress stand between its front door and the edge of the meadow.

'Sometimes I wonder if we *have* got back, it's so well hidden,' Dooley said, as if reading Jude's thoughts. 'Pile off an' cast your saddle, Linsey.'

'What about the horse?'

'Just turn him loose. He ain't goin' anywhere, unless he knows where to look.'

As he unsaddled, Jude realized what it was that the gang had been doing. They'd been working their way up a line of the Great Northern Rail Road, moving the raided gain until it was stockpiled at the top end of the valley. This was where they aimed to settle down, probably live well-thought-of, respectable lives.

Jude freed the roan, watched it wheel and trot into the grass, blowing and heaving as it stretched itself with new-found freedom. The other horses did much the same thing, and then, led by Dooley Susan's clay-bank, they all ran for the nearest spring.

'One day we'll have us a spread up here to rival any o' the big, Bull Chop cattlemen,' Dooley said. 'Go on in, an' see what we started.' Dooley had a small canvas sack of money in each hand now. 'Bart, get the lamps lit. We don't want to trip over anythin'.'

Bart went into the cabin and lit the oil lamps and a few happy jack candles, before Dooley indicated that Jude went ahead of him. Inside, Jude saw that although the green pine-logged, single room was bare-boned, it was large, and made for the improving of. Midway along one side of the room which he estimated to be about thirty feet long, was a wide, rock-built hearth with a deep mantle of cracked ash. It was where, on very cold nights, a warm sleeping bench could be improvised. At either side of the fireplace were large war chests. On top of one, Jude saw cartridge boxes, a Colt revolver and two, big hunting knives.

The small heavy sacks which resembled the ones from the Spooncr's Drift Bank, were tossed on to the rough-puncheoned floor as if they contained nothing more valuable than fir cones.

There were two sets of bunk beds at opposite corners at the back end of the cabin. The saddles and bridles were brought in and hung on wall-driven pegs. Sacks and small boxes of provisions were arranged neatly on the floor either side of the doorway. A side of bacon which still bore its packing-house stamp, hung from one of three overhead beams.

All the bunk blankets were Navaho and bright red and yellow. Two rifles were in a forked rack between the bunks, and a sawn-off shotgun rested at the foot of one of them.

They're expecting some sort of assault, Jude thought. And which was more than likely, he reckoned. 'It must have taken you some time to haul all this stuff up here?' he said with almost genuine interest.

'Yeah it did,' Dooley confirmed. 'It's goin' to be a place worth defendin'.'

Jude wasn't quite sure what Dooley meant, but he didn't ask.

'Don't get tempted by what you see lyin' around,' Bart advised him. 'Unless you fancy your chances with an unloaded gun.'

'Now, why don't you make yourself useful,' Dooley said. 'There's water in the creek, an' you'll need it for cookin' an' washin'.'

Yeah, very amusing, Jude thought unenthusiastically. In staying alive, his chances of getting shot were even greater now he'd accompanied the Susan Boys back to their lair. But if you send someone to watch over me, *he'll* be the one who ain't takin' any supper, he decided.

Ghost was standing in the doorway and he sniggered, shook his head at Dooley's suggestion. 'He ain't that daft,' he said. 'His days are runnin' out, an' he knows it. He'll know what to do with a few yards' start. Anyways, what the hell do we need water for? We got bottles o' snake-head for drinkin'. Fried hog don't need it, an' I ain't scrubbin' up this side o' Christmas.'

As if they needed the warning reminder, Bart and Dese Dawter shared a thoughtful look. Then they collected up the guns and put them in one of the chests.

Dooley opened the lid of the second one and pulled out another brightly coloured blanket. 'Here, take this,' he said to Jude. 'Nights get pretty cold up here.'

'Christ, Dooley, you goin' to read him a bedtime story?' Ghost said, as he sat on the edge of a bunk and started to pull his boots off.

Jude guessed that because they were all so worn

out, he'd probably see the night through. But surely then, his days *would* be numbered. Although Dooley seemed to have something up his sleeve regarding his future, Jude couldn't figure it. Right now, it didn't sound like they even wanted him as cook *or* bottle washer.

'We've still got that sack o' posse gear we borrowed from that sheriff down on the South Fork,' Bart said. 'There's ankle irons an' cuffs in there, an' I reckon they're our boy's fit.'

Then Jude took another stab at why Dooley wanted him there. There is a reason, and it's got to be somethin' to do with movin' stuff from the cabin out to one of the big coastal towns. Yeah, that could be it. He'd be bringing up the rear, a hostage until they'd cleared the mountains. As they travelled west, he'd be their shield from the guns that were surely following. But if he was right, and meantime, he was at least getting a few more hours of survival.

'I'll tell you boys what I'm thinkin',' Ghost said, when the others were lying flat out on their bunks. 'We might be the ones who's wanted, but there's a feller runnin' free who I'd not trust further'n spittin' distance.'

'Yeah, an' we paid him *two thousand dollars*,' Bart said with anger and disgust.

Jude didn't understand who or what they were talking about as he lay in the corner. But he had a hunch. He pulled the blanket around him, and with his head on his flap of his own saddle, he closed his eyes and wondered if his deliberations would allow him a few hours of sleep.

21

For more than four hours, Jude schemed and planned, but only realized failure at the end of each escape plan. Perhaps it's a dawn execution they've got in mind, he considered morbidly. Eventually, he placed his hopes on Pipestone arriving to save him. Pipe dream more likely, he muttered to himself.

As first light eked its way through the narrow windows that were set into the easterly end of the cabin, he shook himself fully alert. He sniffed and coughed. 'Jeeesus' he cursed, drawing his knees up to his chin. 'This place smells worse'n old Ephraim's den. I need to go downstream a bit, take a sluice in the creek, along with other needs. I'd even be happy for someone to attend me,' he said hoarsely.

There was a good ten seconds of silence while the waking men took in what Jude had said. Then Bart let out a low laugh. 'As I said to you before, Linsey, just keep that humour goin'.'

Jude shrugged, thought he'd try a more gritty

response to his predicament. 'Take these goddamn irons off my feet,' he snapped. 'Where the hell do you expect me to go? There ain't even a horse saddled yet.'

Indifferently, Dawter released Jude's irons and removed his wrist cuffs. Jude stamped around, eased some suppleness into his cramping leg muscles.

'I'm goin' outside. Shoot me if you must. I feel half dead already, so bein' back-shot by one o' you can't be much worse,' he challenged.

'I'll go with him,' Dooley said. 'Dese, you, too, keep a look out for Ghost. Whatever the hell he's doin' out there, we don't want him firin' a rifle if there's snoopers gettin' close.'

Jude stopped to look out across the meadow. He saw the roan who stood off forty or fifty feet from the other horses.

'He ain't much of a mixer, is he?' Dooley observed.

Jude shrugged. 'I guess he don't see the point.'

'An' maybe he wants to be left alone, to have the peace an' quiet all to himself,' Dooley offered. 'It's goin' to suit me, spendin' the rest o' my life right here.'

'How does that work then? You, your brother an' a pair o' cat's-paws for company,' Jude said with a mocking smile.

'They'd move on. I'd get me all the devotions of a good woman.'

'Bein' *good* won't have much to do with it. Stayin' up here 'cause you want to's one thing; because you've *got* to's another,' Jude offered. 'It ain't much of a town, but after one winter, a woman who likes her comforts will be drawn to Spooner's Drift like a moth to a candle.'

'Yeah? An' how the hell's she supposed to get down there?'

Jude laughed. 'You're goin' to make one hell of a catch,' he said wearily. 'You got somethin' else you want to say to me? You ain't here to jawbone, or see me wash behind my ears.'

'Yeah, that's true,' Dooley said with a tentative, scheming smile. 'Seein' your roan there, uncertain, just wonderin'. It kinda prompts me to ask.'

'Ask what? I didn't know *askin'* was in your gift.'

'It ain't normally. I was goin' to make an exception in askin' you to join us.'

'Join you?' Jude echoed. 'For Christ's sake I thought you'd brought me out here to shoot me. What the hell makes you think I'd believe that, or even consider it?'

'The money. More dollars than you could stack in a single pile.'

'You mean you ain't goin' to shoot me? Just divi' up your cash pile . . . give me a share to stop me talkin'?'

'No, not quite, Linsey. There's one more raid to carry out. We need another rider.'

'Where? Where's the raid?'

'Down in the Sacramento Valley. A fat cattlemen's bank. Up real close to the foothills. After the robbery, we'd ride into the Sierras, *not* back across the valley. The men – an' that's includin' you – split up. Only *then*, an' takin' your own time, do you make your way back here.'

'Hmm. Knowin' I ain't got any choice, you want to know *now* if I'll join up with you?'

'Sayin' *no's* a choice. It ain't one with prospects, but it's a choice.'

'An' if I did say *no*?'

'You've known the answer to that for some time. The only parts o' you that leave here's in the beaks o' buzzards.'

For the rest of the day, Jude did his best to let the Susan brothers think he was relaxing into the idea of seriously considering their offer.

'I'm goin' to sleep on that offer,' he told Dooley late that night. It was one more attempt at keeping an option alive, and probably himself. He didn't want to alert or alarm them to the fact he was actually about to make a distinctly different play.

The following morning, shortly after Jude had cooked them all fried biscuits and bacon, he approached Ghost Mower, who was standing beside Bart Susan watching the roan.

'You still think you can ride him?' Bart asked Ghost.

'I said I could, didn't I?'

'Yeah, you did, Ghost. What price are you givin'?'

'What price? Why I'll bet any o' you a hundred dollars I can ride him till I'm the one who's ready to step off. To me, that don't seem much more thorny than sittin' in a porch rocker.'

'Yeah, well, it ain't sittin' *in* that's got my interest,' Bart responded. 'I've a hunch about that horse, an' I'll match your wager. What about it?' he said, turning to Linsey. 'You want to go grab the roan an' bring him over? Ghost can set about puttin' his own saddle up.'

'Yeah, I'll do that,' Jude agreed. 'Be just like a real rodeo hittin' town.'

Ten minutes later, Ghost emerged from the cabin. He was toting his own square-skirted saddle and a blanket.

Oh, he's just goin' to love you, feller, Jude thought, when he saw Ghost had put on long-shanked spurs.

Dooley Susan, who had now walked up to the pole fence, didn't appear too concerned either way at Ghost riding Jude's horse. He stretched his arms and yawned, watched impassively, as Ghost slipped the bridle over the roan's head.

Son-of-a-bitch knows as much about horses as a hay waddy, Jude's thoughts continued, as he watched Ghost adjust the headstall, tighten the throat-latch, and trap the fringe of dark, coarse hair under the roan's brow-band. He could now feel his heart thudding faster against his chest. Something was about to happen, and he sensed it was the time for him to take a chance. And where the hell are you, Pipestone? he wondered for the umpteenth time.

Ghost grabbed the saddle by its horn and shook it. 'So, you ain't bettin' against me?' he asked Jude.

'You couldn't cover the wager that says you ain't ever ridin' my horse,' Jude answered with a quiet, cold smile.

Thinking that Ghost might retaliate, Bart edged between them. He was so close, that for a moment, Jude considered making a grab for the man's Colt.

'You know somethin' we don't?' he asked Jude.

'I know somethin' o' the devil's mind. That's what I'm *not* bettin' on.'

Bart considered for a short moment, then he took a step back and nodded acceptingly at his brother. Meanwhile, Dese Dawter had come to watch, was perversely advising Ghost on the safest way to get thrown.

'Shut up, Dese,' Ghost shouted back at him. 'You never got piled from a goddamn puddin' foot. I growed up on bad horses.'

'Lead him out to the grass aways,' Dooley shouted. 'If he's smart, he'll use the fence an' the trees to upset you.'

Ghost took the reins and saddle horn, quickly hauled himself into the saddle. 'I'll ride him my way, boss. No disrespect,' he said.

To Jude's clear surprise, Ghost kicked the roan into a fifty yard run. Standing out in tall meadow grass, the roan stopped, as if he'd admitted the defeat.

'Spur him. Go on Ghost, rowel him,' Bart yelled.

'You ain't gettin' my money that easy.'

Meanwhile, Jude was playing a very edgy game. As if he didn't understand, or was worried about the roan's breaking spirit, he'd withdrawn. He'd dourly dragged his feet to the cypress stand, almost halfway back to the cabin. He groaned, held his breath when he saw Ghost readying himself to rake the roan's belly with the big spurs. Stick him with *them*, an' you'll be buttin' sky, he almost called out.

22

No anxiety was felt for Jude until he'd been gone for three days and nights. Even then, Rachel Fletcher was the first to feel concern. But she kept her fears silent until after the burial of Alice Rickson, whose death had cast a shadow across the Bull Chop.

When Noel Linsey came home at noon, Jude's mother mentioned her own growing concern.

'He'll have gone to the north end of Eel Creek,' Linsey answered.

'For how long though?' Marge Linsey asked her husband.

'As long as it takes him, Mother. He can take care of himself. Pipestone will be back any day now. Let's wait till then.'

Marge didn't seem too mollified by the reasoning.

'Jude's reason for takin' off would be to do some thinkin' about the sheriff's job. You know as well as I do, Mother, Jude's thinkin' usually overcomes any actual doin'. So let's give him some time. The outcome might just be worth it. How's Rachel? She's worried too, I hear.'

'Yes she is. No one seems to know quite why. She didn't lose any money did she, from the bank? That's when she started gettin' funny. She's still actin' like there's a burr under her saddle, Noel.'

'Yeah, I've noticed. But no, she never lost anythin' from the bank.'

The few men in Spooner's Drift who knew about Pipestone and his two deputies had been instrumental in preventing Forbes Rickson from dispatching a force of trigger-happy storekeepers across the Bull Chop valley. But now, they, too, had become apprehensive at the end of another day.

Noel Linsey and Patch Bosun had met Doc Wishnak outside of the courthouse.

'Me an' Patch think we should send out a company o' riders to look for Pipestone,' Linsey said. 'Him, Cappy an' Hank. They should have been back by now, Doc. Bere woulda guessed they were after him, an' laid up an ambush.'

'Well it's possible, but that don't mean probable,' Ralph Wishnak responded. 'He ain't gettin' one up on Pipestone, not in that country. They'll be back. Just give 'em time.'

'Yeah, I been tellin' my missus the same sort o' thing,' Linsey said, but with little conviction.

Later the same afternoon, Pipestone and his two deputized colleagues did return as the doctor said they would. They were dirty and dishevelled, although it showed less on Pipestone's time and weatherworn features.

'Hell, it's like gettin' blood from a stone,' Corbett Welt said about getting information from Pipestone. 'An' neither o' you saw anythin' o' Bere?' he asked.

Rowles and Bowson shook their heads negatively.

'No,' Bosun,' admitted. 'Nothin' to say he was anywhere near us.'

After full dark, when Pipestone, Ralph Wishnak, Noel Linsey and Patch Bosun were together, Pipestone handed over a small canvas sack that he'd kept hidden since riding into town.

'That's the nearest we got to Ingram Bere,' he explained. 'We found it empty, just like his camp. The sign said he hightailed west, but we couldn't've caught him. He had the hours, an' he was makin' miles his priority.'

'So we ain't likely to ever know the real truth about Miss Rickson, or where this coin bag came from?' Bosun suggested.

Pipestone shook his head. 'But we could all take a good stab at guessin'.'

'An' you never saw any sign o' Jude up there?' Jude's father queried.

'No, but I know where he was headed. Just as soon as I've rested my brow for an hour or two, I'll go fetch him. Curious that he ain't back though.'

23

Almost screened by the cypress stand, Jude cursed as Ghost Mower kick-spurred the roan. Now he'd find out if his horse was full saddle-broke, or still half wild.

As Ghost's spurs bit its belly, the roan went into the air, as Jude knew it would. The horse humped its back, bent its head down between its forelegs.

Jude swore quietly as he edged further towards the cabin. 'Go on, feller,' he hissed. 'I should never've doubted you. Just keep 'em all amused.'

The roan made a half spin before it hit the ground with its hoofs bunched. Then it was in the air again, dropping back to jar Ghost's backbone with shocking violence.

'Look at the goddamn devil buck,' Bart Susan gasped. 'Ghost ain't ever rode anythin' like that.'

'An' he ain't goin' to,' Dooley said thoughtfully, and looked anxiously towards his brother. 'Look at him, he's turnin' like an auger.'

'Ghost!' Bart yelled across the meadow. 'Pull

goddamn leather if you want. Forget the bet.'

'Get off him an' run, or he'll break you in pieces,' Dese joined in. 'Hell, Linsey never told us the horse was a killer.'

Instinctively, Dese turned around as he spoke; the same chance moment that Jude stepped out from the cabin. He was carrying his Colt in his left hand, a Winchester was levelled out in his right.

Dese cursed, yanked at the pistol he was carrying in the waistband of his pants. 'Dooley, Bart, look out,' he yelled. 'It's Linsey.'

Dese realized his mistake in shouting, but it was too late. Jude brought the Winchester tight into his hip and shot him. With a bullet in the middle of his chest, Dese raised imploring arms and staggered one step forward, but Jude was already turning away as the man died.

One-handed, Jude levered another round into the rifle's firing chamber. He pulled the trigger as Bart Susan brought up his own Colt. There was an explosion of bone and blood as Jude's second bullet smashed its way into his wrist. Bart snatched uselessly for the gun with his good hand, groaned as the pain detonated through his body. Quickly, Jude fired again, saw Bart jerk as the rifle bullet smashed between his shoulder blades. Bart shouted his brother's name as he crumpled sideways, then his body twisted and pressed his face to the hard ground.

'I'll take him, Bart,' Dooley shouted, shooting

twice as Jude ran into the cover of the cypresses.

Jude pressed his shoulders up tight to the hard bark and counted off ten long seconds. Then he dropped his Colt, let his legs collapse under him and went into a low roll away from the bole of the tree. He looked up and saw that Dooley Susan was less than thirty feet away. He was coming towards him, the determination clear in his heavy run.

Jude wanted to shout, 'It's dead or alive', but the words stuck in his throat.

Dooley's eyes were suddenly spoiled with fear, and he veered to one side as he ran. But Jude had little choice. He knew that from Dooley Susan's standpoint, being the only gang member to be captured alive, was insufferable. He brought up the rifle, held just a moment before squeezing off another lethal shot.

Dooley was tough. With a bullet low in the belly, he managed to drag himself on to all fours and raise his dark features. 'Why? You could've joined us,' he wheezed, as their eyes met.

Jude flicked a glance out to the meadow. He saw that Ghost Mower still trying to gain control of the roan, and he looked back at Dooley.

'Your brother lied when he said you weren't killers,' he rasped angrily. 'You *are*, an' would have been again.'

But Dooley's eyes went clouded and sightless as his body collapsed into an insensible heap. The man's chin hit the ground with such force that it snapped back, the dead eyes boring deep into Jude's consciousness.

Jude stepped back to pick up his Colt. He knew that what was happening wasn't his fault or of his choice; they'd left him none. Methodically, he levered another cartridge into the rifle and looked desolately around him. In less than sixty seconds he'd shot and killed the Susan brothers and Dese Dawter. He turned and pointed his rifle out towards the fourth member of the gang.

'Go on then,' he yelled at the roan. 'Don't leave it all to me; throw the bastard.' Jude was gripped with dread as, tormented by the gunfire, the roan suddenly came at the gallop towards him.

Ghost hauled in on the reins, kicked through the pole fence and tried to spur the roan towards the cabin. He'd pulled one of his two Colts, was trying to aim at Jude. He fired off one shot, then another, but the pitch and swerve of the outlaw horse sent the bullets far wide of where Jude was standing stubbornly.

Ghost Mower was now trying to get himself out of the saddle, but with one hand grasping the reins and the other the butt of his Colt, it was too much for him.

Jude lowered the barrel of the rifle. He watched awestruck at the ferocity with which the roan was bucking, its rearing and pawing of the air. Then the horse leaped ahead so aggressively, that Ghost dropped the Colt from his hand. Now he was using both hands in a frantic attempt to stay in the saddle.

'You're *goin'* to bleed from more goddamn places than I got bullets left,' Jude muttered numbly.

The roan whirled again, pitched and backed up, shook himself violently. He went into the air, twisted half round and Ghost fought to claw leather and get a hold. But his hands slipped, and the roan finally wrenched itself from under him.

As if he was done and knew it, the roan ceased bucking, swung its dark head to take a look at the crumpled man at its feet. Then, realizing that Ghost still had one boot in the stirrup, it snorted, stomped and whirled.

'No, just stay,' Jude yelled. 'I'm comin' to cut him loose.'

But the roan had suffered in the last few days. It had no idea of what was happening, the torment was too much. It had one long accusing look at Jude, then lashed back at Ghost with a big, front hoof.

Jude, swung up the Winchester and took aim. 'Goddamn, you wayward devil,' he said, before pulling the trigger one more time.

The roan's front legs buckled, and, killed with the single well-aimed bullet, it fell heavily to the ground.

'No one's give me options,' Jude reasoned quietly, as he leaned the rifle against a cypress. 'I couldn't let you kick him to death,' he said, as he walked slowly to the stricken roan. 'Who'd it have been next time? Maybe Leo Grainger should've turned you loose months back.'

Jude couldn't tell whether it was the roan's hoof, or whether Ghost's neck had been broken when he'd fallen from the saddle. 'Don't much matter,' he said, tired and stoical. He pulled Ghost's foot from the stirrup and dragged him into the shade of the trees. He wiped his shirt sleeve across his sweat-grimed face and made a quick survey of the other members of the gang. 'Now I know what dust to dust, means,' he figured out on seeing a distant lark rise. 'An' you can have your meadow back.'

24

An hour later, Jude had dragged the dead men around to the back wall of the cabin. He laid them side by side and draped a tarpaulin over them. The bodies would fetch a thousand dollars each; the price that Odgen Sayler had pledged.

Jude went to the roan and removed the saddle. He carried it into the cabin, put it just inside of the door, and draped the bridle over it.

More than ten thousand dollars worth of assorted gleaming coin lay under the blanket of Dooley Susan's bunk. Jude extricated canvas bags from under the other bunks and placed them on the table. There was $150,000, give or take a hundred or two, and $30,000 of it was greenback folding currency. Jude's caustic thought was, that up to when you got shot dead, banditry was big business.

There was another small sack at the bottom of one of the two upper bunks, and Jude emptied its contents on the table. He turned over watches, silver and gold cases, chains and an assortment of rings, guessed the haul was the contents of a few banks' safety deposit boxes.

As the hours passed, Jude was resigned to wait at least until the following day. He knew that Pipestone would come sooner or later. The old frontiersman wouldn't let him down, he'd be thinking of Jude's fishing trip, and those two 'grizzlies' he'd spoken of.

When first dark arrived, ten gorged buzzards dragged their heavy bodies away from the carcass of Jude's dead roan. 'Huh. It's an ill wind that's blown across this section o' the Bull Chop,' he mumbled, a bit mawkish after consuming a half-bottle of the gang's snake-head whiskey.

Leaving the door and one of the windows open, Jude wearily pulled off his boots and socks and stretched out on the bunk with the stashed hoard under it. Close to the weak light from a guttering, breeze-blown candle, he lifted a folded copy of the *Tehama Examiner* from a narrow shelf that ran above his head. 'Gather round, boys,' he addressed the night critters that he thought would be scratching around the floor of the cabin. 'Gather round, an' I'll read you about another sort o' life.' After a minute, he realized he couldn't read or concentrate on printed words, and he let the newspaper drop to the floor.

'For Christ's sake, hurry up, Pipestone,' he repeated.

*

Well after daybreak the following morning, Jude raised his head from the rolled blanket. He blinked and rubbed his eyes, wondered where the sound was coming from.

'Jude, Jude Linsey, you hidin' up in there?' Pipestone was calling out, from the far side of the cypress stand.

'Yeah, I'm here,' Jude rasped. 'What the hell kept you?'

Pipestone swung down from his mule, ambled on up to the cabin and poked his head through the open doorway. 'I saw 'em comin' down from way back ... thought maybe it was your hide them buzzards were feastin' off,' the old mountain man said and chuckled.

'Well, now you seen it ain't,' Jude responded with a measure of bitterness.

'Looks like I finally managed to creep up on you. Are you goin' to waste *all* o' this day?'

'Some of it I'd like to, yeah,' Jude mumbled drily. 'Thanks for wakin' me, Pipe. *This* time, I really did have somethin' else on my mind.'

'Yeah, reckon I know what you might've been dreamin' on. I've already rode around your own little Boot Hill. That's some handiwork, kid.'

'Huh. It looks like you were right when you said they were ridin' the Bull Chop,' Jude said. 'They never ever left the valley.'

'Yep. It might've been years before anyone ever got up here. There weren't much to follow, not even for a trace nose like mine,' Pipestone replied. 'Was it *you* shot the roan? Or what's left of it?'

Jude swung his legs down and reached for his socks. 'Yeah. I don't think he'd ever have got near to bein' civilized.'

'Not like us, eh?' Pipestone responded ironically. Then he nodded at the hanging side of bacon. 'I'll take me three or four fried slices o' the old pig, when you're ready,' he said. 'That's store meat that I ain't tasted the like of in many a moon.'

Jude was stamping a heel into a boot. 'I was beginnin' to think you'd never come,' he said.

'I was only doin' what I was asked to do. I came as soon as I could, young feller. We was chasin' Bere, but after what he did to the girl, he was sure mixin' his sign. We had no alternative but to rein in on the chase. We'd never've caught him.'

Jude thought for a moment. 'What girl?' he asked with quick, mounting unease. 'What girl are you talkin' about?'

Pipestone shook his old head, puffed wretchedly. 'Sorry, Jude, I didn't think. You had no way o' knowin', did you? It was the Rickson girl . . . Alice. It looked like she met up with Bere, an' somehow she got herself shot . . . killed.'

Jude walked quietly out to the meadow, stared long and hard into the distance. Pipestone let him be, thought maybe he understood the enormity of Jude's thinking, even considering for the future.

Fifteen minutes later, Jude came back, his face

drawn, set impassively. 'Where'd you reckon Bere was headed?' he asked, and it was clear he wanted a *good* reckoning.

'West. An' that's where I'd go, if I wanted to go missin'. It was no good goin' after him, Jude. He'd got too big a lead on us, an' he weren't goin' to slow down.'

'Yeah, OK. I guess he'll keep,' Jude said, as if for his own account. 'Can you help me look those fellers over?' he asked. 'Shortly, they ain't goin' to be much fun to handle. Not if we ain't vultures.'

In Pipestone and Jude's search of the men's clothing, they found an assortment of gewgaws and personal trinkets. A lot of the stuff was the obvious pickings of hold-ups along the route of the rail line.

'This one's carryin' letters,' Pipestone said. 'You want I should read 'em?'

'You can't. Let me see.'

Jude sat on the cabin doorsill, read the papers from Dooley Susan's pocket. 'These letters are to Bart an' Dooley Susan, both. They look first off as though they're from their ma, but they're not,' he said, after a couple of minutes. 'A ma would call herself ma, or mother. They're just signed with an R. Sounds more like a sister,' he reasoned, and looked again at the envelopes. 'This one's addressed care o' the ticket office at Oakland, an' it's postmarked nearly a year gone. But this one's to Red Bluff, an' it was mailed in Spooner's Drift, less than three weeks ago.'

Pipestone pulled off his tatty coonskin cap hat and scratched his head. 'Who in tarnation's writin' to the Susans from Spooners' Drift, Jude? We'd know 'em.'

'We do. It's Rachel Fletcher. Two o' them fellers I shot dead an' aim to leave as goddamn buzzard meat, are her brothers.'

'I guess it makes some sense of her feelins' then – why she wanted to know about what they'd done – the folk they'd shot an' killed. Imagine havin' them two sons o' bitches as kin.

Jude sat with scalding, strong coffee while Pipestone chomped on hot bacon slices.

'Our good sheriff was workin' with the gang?' Jude put forward.

'By the time they got this far north, he was,' Pipestone grunted out between bites. 'They could've shot *him* when he gave chase with the others. But they didn't.'

'No, Saul Pruitt caught it instead,' Jude recalled, with mixed emotions. 'An' after that?'

'They would've paid him off. They could afford it.'

'So, what of Alice?'

'Who knows? Because there ain't much else to go on, I'm guessin' he wanted to propositon her. Heaven knows what he coulda been offerin', but she must've rejected it, an' he took it badly. Will Lasseter said it weren't no love nest he found. I'm sorry, Jude. What are you goin' to do now?'

'Load up the horses to take all this stuff back. I know most folk'll be relieved to see the return o' their money, regardless o' the cost.' Jude swirled his coffee around the tin mug. 'Dooley said he was goin' to be happy up here, so *here* he can stay, along with the rest of his gang. I'll go home, then see Rachel. The ride back'll give me time to work out what I'm goin' to say to her. Whatever it is, I don't see myself comin' out of it too well. Second thing's to put Cappy Rowles in charge, 'cause I'll be headed west.'

Jude was thinking, wondering if Alice had died still unaware of why he'd not ridden out with the sheriff's posse. 'I'll cross the South Fork . . . ride to the ocean if I have to,' was his menacing pledge. 'Ingram Bere's runnin' from what he did, but whatever path he's on, it ain't goin' to be long enough or dark enough.'

Pipestone wiped the bacon fat from around his whiskery chops. 'It won't be *you* fillin' the sheriff's chair, then?'

'No, I'm not ready yet for doin' this sort o' thing, lawful or otherwise. But if that badge is still available, I'll be takin' it with me. I'm goin' to pin it back on him personal.'

A mean grin broke across Pipestone's face. 'You think you'll get close enough to do that?' he said.

Jude nodded. 'Yeah, just after I've shot him,' he replied sternly.

With his forefinger, Pipestone marked a greasy line across the table top. 'This side o' the South Fork, there's worked-out silver mines that pock the timber-

line,' he said. 'If I was Bere, I'd climb into one . . .
stay real quiet until anyone followin' had passed by,'
he offered Jude as guidance.

25

Jude was two days' ride west of the Bull Chop. He was looking out from Eagle Peak, where dense timber drifted down to the South Fork River. It was where, many years before, a string of small claims had been tunnelled into the rocky escarpment below the timberline. He'd dismounted to lead the mare in a zigzag along the broken boundary of trees. Every few steps he whispered soothing noises, held the palm of his hand to the horse's nostrils.

It was from just beyond where trees broke into the open land, that Jude had seen the movement. He wanted to cut off any retreat that Ingram Bere could make into the cover of the timber. But, as he shifted position, the mare stumbled and its front hoofs made a cascade of loose scree. In the still, silent air the noise was enough to startle the nervous, ever-watchful Bere. The man grabbed for his Colt, turned to see the indistinct and silhouetted figure of Jude who'd led his horse out of the trees.

The man had been to the creek, now Jude was offering little option but for him to get back to the portal of the old silver mine. 'Got him. There's just some things you don't do on your doorstep,' he seethed with satisfaction. He moved quickly to one side and fired off two shots. But they were meant to miss. He wanted to be close, wanted to see Bere's face when he took him.

Bere issued a string of curses as he scrambled for cover. He twisted one way then the other, his eyes estimating the distances between the man bearing down on him and the safety of his hiding camp. Although Jude was fast approaching him, he had no idea of his identity, or how many of them there were. It was only the gut-wrenching certainty of their intent that made him pick up and run faster.

When Bere made it to the mine's entrance, he turned, fired once back at Jude's running figure, then vanished into the protection of the tunnel.

Jude shook his head at the blunder he'd prompted Bere to make. Now the one-time Sheriff of Spooner's Drift was cornered, and Jude cautiously edged to one side as he stepped up the overgrown threshold.

A bullet exploded into a side timber and Jude flinched. But, at the the sound of running feet, he darted into the dark hole of the shaft and levelled his Colt. He listened carefully as his eyes adjusted to the blackness. He could hear Bere moving ahead of him, but he couldn't be sure how far into the mine he'd gone. He moved forward carefully until the entrance was a faint glimmer of light at his back, then he moved away from the wall. Now he could make out more of the surroundings. It was like Pipestone had said; the mine had obviously been worked out, had remained abandoned for years. The prop timbers were chewed with decay and cobwebs blanketed thickly where they angled into the roof. Around him, he could hear soft scuttering, and he shuddered at the glimmer of yellow eyes that backed off from his wary footfalls.

Jude reloaded, thumbed two fresh cartridges into his Colt. 'You found your way home, Bere,' he shouted, as an almost involuntary response. 'It's the rat hole you must've come from.'

'Who the hell *are* you?' the man yelled back after a moment's pause.

Bere's response gave Jude the information he'd wanted, and he hunkered low. 'Unless you got another way out o' this, you just walked into your own grave.'

There was a moment's silence then Bere gave a nervy, faltering laugh. He fired again, dislodged a shard of rotten planking from the roof. 'I asked you your name, feller,' he rasped. 'Seems you gone an' made a mighty big mistake. I'm totin' a star.'

Jude's lips twisted into a dour grimace. 'You ain't carryin' any such thing. Alice Rickson snatched it from you before you killed her. I've got it here, an' I'm just about ready to pin it to your sick, miserable hide.'

Jude was moving resolutely further down the shaft when Bere shouted.

'Jude Linsey,' he hissed back in recognition. 'I should've known.'

'Yeah, an' it's goin' to be the death o' you,' Jude shouted out his words of vengeance, and triggered the Colt twice, then a third time.

The heavy bullets crashed and ricocheted away, and again, Jude spread himself flat against the wall of the shaft. Bere's Colts flashed out of the darkness, pounded bullets from the walls close to where Jude was standing. Jude cursed silently, then ran towards the muzzle flashes. This time a single shot lit up Bere's dark, sneering face, thirty feet ahead of him and he threw himself to the floor. The bullet tore at Jude's shirt sleeve and he stumbled to his knees. But he'd got what he wanted; an after image that burned into his mind.

From his second Colt, Bere pumped more bullets out ahead of him. Jude held his breath in the mad onslaught and fired carefully. He inched forward, and Bere's Colt exploded again. In the flash of light, Jude saw the trapped man clearly. He was hit, with one arm hanging uselessly at his side. Clumsy with pain, his other hand was clawing at the hammer of his Colt.

Jude rolled on to his side and levelled his arms out

full stretch. He gripped his gun in both hands, squeezed off a final shot, even as he saw the barrel of Bere's Colt being raised.

But the sound of both gunshots were accompanied by another more ominous sound.

All around him, Jude heard the old mine shaft groan, as props creaked and buckled. The pulsed explosions of the gunfire had been too much for the shoring timbers that had never been replaced or maintained. Under the weight pressing on them, the ceiling boards started to disintegrate and the unrestrained earth avalanched down.

The last thing Jude saw was the blood and dirt-smeared figure of Ingram Bere. The injured man was staring at the roof of the shaft; stricken with fear as it opened above his head like the jaws of a python about to swallow its rat.

Jude's thwarted curse was bitten off by the dust rot that clogged his throat, and he covered his head with his arms and snarled his frustration. Then a falling cross beam hit him hard between his shoulder blades and knocked him to the ground. He gasped and coughed, felt the acrid dust biting his lungs as he got back to his feet and staggered sideways. But there was a grey, gloomy ball of light behind him, and he knew there must still be an exit from the mine. He brought out the sheriff's badge that Alice had snatched from Bere's shirt front, turned it once in his fingers and tossed it through the billowing cloud.

'It ain't the way either of us would've wanted it,' he said and spat more sour dirt from his mouth.